*"Alicia, are you glad you stayed?"*
*Pierce asked softly.*

Shadows kept her from seeing his face, which was just as well. Longing and desire were nakedly apparent.

"Yes." She tried to sound cheerful and bright. Instead, she sounded breathless and aroused and languorous.

"Good," he said, nodding slowly. "Good."

The way he said it made her throat go dry. There was no moisture with which to wet her lower lip when she dragged her tongue along it.

"Are you coming in? Shall I turn off the lights?" She could scarcely form the words.

Pierce shook his head. "No. I'll be in shortly."

The screen door closed behind her and he heard her soft tread on the stairs to the sleeping loft. He could still smell her hair, still see her eyes reflecting the moonlight.

He didn't follow her in because he knew if he did, he couldn't have stopped himself from taking her in his arms, kissing her deeply and without restraint, touching her, tasting her, and making her his. . . .

# WHAT ARE *LOVESWEPT* ROMANCES?

They are stories of true romance and touching emotion. We believe those two very important ingredients are constants in our highly sensual and very believable stories in the *LOVESWEPT* line. Our goal is to give you, the reader, stories of consistently high quality that may sometimes make you laugh, sometimes make you cry, but are always fresh and creative and contain many delightful surprises within their pages.

Most romance fans read an enormous number of books. Those they truly love, they keep. Others may be traded with friends and soon forgotten. We hope that each *LOVESWEPT* romance will be a treasure—a "keeper." We will always try to publish

*LOVE STORIES YOU'LL NEVER FORGET*
*BY AUTHORS YOU'LL ALWAYS REMEMBER*

The Editors

*LOVESWEPT • 51*

# Sandra Brown
# Send No Flowers

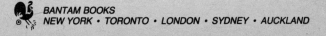
*BANTAM BOOKS*
*NEW YORK • TORONTO • LONDON • SYDNEY • AUCKLAND*

SEND NO FLOWERS

*A Bantam Book / July 1984*

LOVESWEPT® *and the wave device are registered trademarks*
*of Bantam Books, a division of Bantam Doubleday Dell*
*Publishing Group, Inc. Registered in U.S. Patent and*
*Trademark Office and elsewhere.*

*If you would be interested in receiving protective vinyl covers*
*for your Loveswept books, please write to this address*
*for information:*
*Loveswept*
*Bantam Books*
*P. O. Box 985*
*Hicksville, NY 11802*

ISBN 0-553-21659-7

*Published simultaneously in the United States and Canada*

*Bantam Books are published by Bantam Books, a division of*
*Bantam Doubleday Dell Publishing Group, Inc. Its trademark,*
*consisting of the words "Bantam Books" and the portrayal of a*
*rooster, is Registered in U.S. Patent and Trademark Office and in*
*other countries. Marca Registrada. Bantam Books, 666 Fifth*
*Avenue, New York, New York 10103.*

PRINTED IN THE UNITED STATES OF AMERICA

O     11  10  9  8  7  6  5  4  3  2

# One

It was probably the cutest tush he had ever seen.

Through the screen door he had an unrestricted view of it, a derrière roundly feminine, but trim. The cut-off jeans were tight. Denim fringe, bleached and curled from years of laundering, clung damply to taut, slender thighs.

She was on hands and knees, peering into and hesitantly poking at the fuse box near the baseboard. As she leaned down farther to investigate the intricacies of the switches, the man smiled a slow, cat-with-mouse-trapped smile of masculine pleasure. It was the smile of a gratified voyeur. He was a little ashamed of himself. But not ashamed enough to stop looking.

The cabin was dark. Her flashlight gave off a meager glow. The only real illumination came from fierce flashes of blue-white lightning.

The two young boys watching her efforts were growing increasingly restless.

"I'm hungry. You said we'd eat as soon as we got here."

"Do you know how to turn the lights on, Mom? I bet you don't."

The man at the door saw her head fall forward between her shoulders in an attitude of defeat. It lasted for only a moment. She raised her head determinedly as she drew in a deep breath. "It's just a fuse box, David. When I find the breaker switch, the electricity will come back on. It must have been tripped by the storm. And, Adam, we'll eat as soon as I can get the lights on and unload the car."

"You said the cabin was gonna be great. I think it stinks," David complained. "We should've used tents."

"Yeah, tents," the younger brother seconded.

"If you don't think I can turn on the breaker switch, what makes you think I could put up a tent?"

The rising impatience in the young woman's voice was unmistakable and the man at the door didn't blame her for it. But the two little boys looked so bedraggled that he couldn't blame them for their complaining either. They were only kids and had apparently spent hours traveling. Their arrival at the lake cabin had been inauspicious to say the least.

He had seen the headlights of their car when they arrived. A few minutes later, he decided to brave one of the most tumultuous thunderstorms he remembered in recent history and walk to the cabin only a hundred yards from his. That hundred yards was through dense woods which guaranteed the owners of the cabins privacy. Walking through it in a thunderstorm had been foolhardy, but he had become concerned for his neighbors. His electricity had gone out about ten minutes before their arrival and God knew when it would come back on.

Now as he listened to the whining of the boys and the near desperation in the young woman's voice he was glad he had chanced the woods. She needed help and she was alone. At least there was no husband and father in evidence.

"We should've stopped at Burger Town. David and I wanted to eat there, didn't we, David?"

"I knew this was gonna be a jerky camping trip. I wanted to use a tent and camp for real, not stay in a dumb cabin."

The young woman raised up to sit on her heels, hands on hips. "Well if you're such a pioneer, you can go out in the rain and start hunting or fishing for our supper." The boys fell silent. "I've had it with you two. Do you hear me? This cabin was graciously loaned to us. Since we don't have a tent and know nothing about them, I thought it was best we take up the offer to use it. I can't do anything about the storm. But I'm trying my best to get the electricity back on. Now stop the complaining!" She matched her stern tone with an intimidating glare and returned to her fanny-in-the-air position to futilely inspect the fuse box.

Glumly the brothers looked at each other and shook their heads. They were convinced their trip was doomed to disaster. "Do you think she can fix the 'lectricity?" the younger asked the older in a loud whisper.

"No, do you?"

"No."

Now was the time to make his presence known. He had never been a window peeper and was ashamed for having stood outside this long without letting them know he was there. But he was enjoying them. They were in no immediate danger. Their tribulation somehow endeared them to him. He found himself smiling at the comments of the two boys and the parental frustration of the woman. Maybe watching their dilemma was acting as a panacea for his own. Observing them had certainly taken his mind off his problem. Albeit unfair, that was human nature.

It was also human nature for him to feel a shaft of desire spear through him each time he gazed at the display of long bare thighs and that incredibly delectable tush. That wasn't fair either. It was downright lechery to lust after a wife as well as the mother of two young boys. But could a man be held responsible for his thoughts?

"Mom, I have to go to the bathroom." It was Adam who spoke.

"Number one or number two?"

"Number one. Bad."

"Well, since we haven't located the bathroom yet, go outside."

"It's raining."

"I know that, Adam," she said with diminishing patience. "Stand on the porch under the roof and aim out."

"Okay," he mumbled and turned toward the door. "Hey, Mom."

"Hmm?" She was dickering with one of the switches.

"There's a man out there."

The young woman spun around, toppled backward, and gasped in alarm, "A *man*?"

Quickly, hoping not to frighten her, he switched on his high-beam flashlight and caught in its paralyzing spotlight an impressive chest straining against a chambray workshirt tied in a knot at her waist, a tumble of blond hair that had escaped a haphazard ponytail, and wide blue eyes.

Alicia Russell gulped in air and held it, her heart pounding. A brilliant flash of lightning silhouetted him where he stood just outside the screen door. Had she locked it behind them? Would it matter? He looked huge and fearsome against the stormy sky. And he was coming in!

He pulled the screen door open. It was ripped from his hand by the force of the wind and crashed against the outside wall. She and the boys cowered. He rushed across the room and dropped to his knees in front of her where she was sprawled. Her eyes were blinded by his flashlight. She could no longer see him except as a looming hulk bending over her. She opened her mouth to scream for her boys to run.

"Are you all right?" He switched off the light and for a moment everything was black. "I didn't mean to scare you. Here, let me help you up."

Alicia recoiled and the hand extended to her was withdrawn.

"I'm f-fine," she stuttered. "Startled, that's all." She pulled herself to her feet without his assistance. Her first concern was for her sons who were eyeing the stranger curiously. "David, go help Adam . . . uh . . . do what he has to do on the porch." If she was going to be raped and murdered, she didn't want her sons to witness it. God, where was the telephone? Why didn't the lights come back on? Who was this man and where had he come from? Her heart was banging against her ribs and pounding on the inside of her eardrums.

"Hi," David chirped. Alicia cursed herself for teaching her children to be courteous and friendly. "I'm David. This is Adam. I'm the oldest."

"Hello," the man said. Alicia thought he smiled, but it was so dark, she couldn't tell. Her flashlight had flickered out and he had kept his turned off. "My name is Pierce."

"David—" Alicia began, only to be interrupted by her eldest.

"We're gonna camp here for a week, but Mom can't turn the lights on. She's not too good at things like that."

The stranger looked in her direction, then back down at the boys. "Few moms are. But she couldn't have turned the lights on anyway. The power's off because of the storm."

"Da-vid," Alicia ground out through gritted teeth.

"Why don't you take your brother outside," the stranger suggested, "while I see if I can help your mom."

"Okay. Come on, Adam."

The screen door slammed behind them and the man turned to Alicia. "You're off to a bad beginning. The campers aren't too happy."

If he were a rapist and murderer, he was a polite one. But then it was said the Boston strangler had been too. And Jack the Ripper. "I'm sure once the electricity comes back on and they get something to eat, they'll be in a better frame of mind." There, that sounded good. Unafraid, in control, cool, calm, capable.

"Where are your lanterns? I'll light them for you."

So much for cool, calm, and capable. "Lanterns?" Employing that gesture that is universally used by women to give them an air of indifference and make them appear less stupid than they feel at the given moment, she reached up and made patting, straightening motions on her hair. She also gave the frayed hem of her cut-offs a swift, hard tug. "I don't know. The cabin is borrowed and I didn't have a chance to look around."

"Candles?"

She shook her head.

"You didn't bring any emergency equipment with you?"

"No, I didn't," she snapped testily, hating the incredulity in his voice. It made her feel imbecilic. This was the first camping attempt she had braved with her sons. How good was she supposed to be the first time out? "We'll be fine when the power comes back on."

"Why don't you wait out the storm in my cabin? We'll have to walk through the woods, but it's not far."

"No," she rushed to say. He had made her feel even

more incompetent than she already did. That irritation had taken her mind off the possible danger he posed. But her panic quickly resurfaced when he mentioned their going to his cabin.

"That only makes sense. I can cook something for the boys on a butane stove."

"No, really, Mr. . . . uh . . ."

"Pierce."

"Thank you, Mr. Pierce, but—"

"No, Pierce is my first name. Pierce Reynolds."

"Mr. Reynolds, we'll manage. I don't want to leave the cabin."

"Why?"

She could hear the boys playing on the front porch, letting the rainwater splash on the palms they extended past the overhang. "My . . . my husband plans to join us later tonight. We should be here when he arrives or he'll be worried."

"Oh." He rubbed the back of his neck in indecision. "I hate to leave you alone under the circumstances. Why don't we leave him a note and tell him where you are?"

"Hey, Mom, we're starving," David said. He and Adam had tired of the game and trooped back inside. "When can we eat?"

"We're starving," Adam echoed.

"I really think it would be best if you came to my cabin."

"I—"

Before Alicia had a chance to object the man turned to the two boys. "How does chili sound? If you come back to my cabin with me, I can have it heated up in no time."

"Gee, neat. That'd be great," David said enthusiastically.

"Neat," Adam said.

"But you'll have to walk through the woods to get

there," the man warned. "There's no road to drive your car through."

"We don't mind, do we, Adam?" They were already racing toward the screen door.

"Boys!" Alicia called after them frantically, but they heedlessly dashed outside.

"Come on, Mrs—?"

"Russell."

"Mrs. Russell. I can't leave you and the boys here alone. I promise I'm not someone you need to be afraid of."

Just then another flash of lightning rent the sky in two. Alicia thought the prospect of the power being restored was nil. She had been an idiot not to come prepared for something like this, but it was too late to do anything about it now. At least the boys could be fed. When the rain abated, they could come back and wait for morning.

With a resigned sigh and a prayer that she could trust this man with her virtue and their lives, she said, "All right." The only thing she took with her was her purse. It would be insane to unload their bags from the car in the downpour.

On the front porch, Pierce Reynolds lifted Adam into his arms and directed David to take his mother's hand. "Okay, everybody, hold on tight. Mrs. Russell." For a long moment, Alicia stared down at the strong, lean hand extended to her. Then she placed her hand against it and he clasped it tightly.

The rain drove against them like stinging needles. Wind tore at their hair and clothes and buffeted them about. Each time lightning flashed, Adam buried his face deeper into Mr. Reynold's neck. David tried his best to be valiant, but he was fearfully clinging to Alicia by the time they saw the other cabin through the trees.

"Almost there, troops," Mr. Reynolds called over the roar of the storm.

They reached the security of the covered porch just as a clap of thunder rattled the window panes. "Let's leave our shoes out here," Pierce said, setting Adam down. When they were all barefoot, he led them through the front door of the cabin that was softly lit by two kerosene lanterns and smoldering coals in the fireplace.

"I'm cold. How about everyone else?" Pierce crossed the room and knelt in front of the fireplace to stir the logs with a poker. Glancing over his shoulder, he saw his three guests huddling uncertainly just inside the threshold. They were shivering. "David, bring me one of those logs, please." The boy picked a log from the box near the door and rushed it to the man who was definitely hero-material. "Thanks." Pierce ruffled the boy's wet hair. "You'll find towels for you and Adam and your mother in the bathroom."

"Yes, sir," David said and ran toward the door that could only lead to the bathroom. The cabin was one large room serving as living room, bedroom, dining room, and kitchen. Comfortable chairs and a sofa were arranged in front of the fireplace. A double bed was tucked under a drastically sloping ceiling, which was actually the bottom of a narrow staircase that led up to a sleeping loft. It was too homey to be rustic and was spotlessly clean.

David emerged from the bathroom carrying a stack of folded towels. After first handing one to Pierce, he took them to his mother and brother. Alicia felt a sense of unreality. What was she doing here in this stranger's mountain retreat, alone with him in a veritable wilderness? It would have been bad enough if he were old and feeble, or kindly but pitifully ugly and ignorant. But their rescuer was handsome and suave and virile, something she hadn't known until they entered the cabin and she had seen him in the light.

His hair was ash brown, and threaded with silver. It was carefully cut to look carelessly styled and was worn a trifle longer than fashion currently dictated. When he had turned his head Alicia had seen green eyes as brilliant as emeralds beneath a shelf of masculine brows. As he added the log to the coals and fanned it to life, well-developed muscles rippled beneath his wet cotton shirt, though his physique wasn't brawny.

He made her inordinately nervous. Not because she thought he would harm them. No man who would carry a little boy through a thunderstorm, murmuring reassurances that there was nothing to be afraid of, could be a murderer. As for being a rapist . . . Well, it was clear he would never have to *force* any woman.

"I'm glad I decided to build a fire earlier tonight. It was barely cool enough then, but now—"

Pierce stopped mid-sentence. Because if Alicia was surprised to find him so appealingly attractive, her reaction to him couldn't compare to the explosion in his chest and loins when he stood and turned to face her. Her hair was wet and silkily draping her cheeks, neck, and shoulders. The chambray was soaked and plastered against full breasts and nipples peaked hard from the cold. He had a helluva time keeping his eyes off them. Her bare feet only made her legs look longer and shapelier. They were covered with goose flesh he craved to warm with caressing hands.

He dragged his eyes away from her, cursing himself and this sudden attack of rampant desire. He hadn't felt so compulsively desirous of a woman since . . . He had *never* felt so compulsively desirous of a woman. It baffled him. She was a wife and mother and doing absolutely nothing to entice him. In fact, she looked jittery and nervous, and if his expression revealed anything of what was going on between his thighs, he didn't blame her.

"I think we ought to get you out of those wet clothes. Why don't you take the boys into the bathroom and I'll see if I can find them something to wear."

"All right." Alicia herded her sons toward the sanctity of the bathroom where she hoped she could will her breasts back into a state of repose. He had noticed her distended nipples. She knew he had.

Several minutes later he knocked on the door, though it stood open to give them light. Adam and David had been stripped down to their underpants and Alicia was rubbing them with towels. "Chili is on the stove and I found these in a drawer." He held up two UCLA T-shirts.

"Super," David said, grabbing one and pulling it on over his head. It hung to his knees.

"Say thank you, David, to Mr. Reynolds for loaning you his shirt." She stood slowly, still painfully aware of her wet shirt and short cut-offs. When she had left Los Angeles that afternoon they were enjoying an unseasonable warm spell. For an automobile trip to the woods with David and Adam, the old cut-offs and shirt had seemed like the perfect outfit.

"Thanks, Mr. Reynolds," David said as he helped Adam with his shirt. The hem came to Adam's ankles.

"You're welcome, but the shirts aren't mine. This cabin belongs to my company. Everyone uses it and leaves things behind. I'm sure they'd never be missed if you want to keep them."

"Gee, can we?" The boys raced out looking like two friends of Casper the Ghost. They were happy now that they were warm and dry and dinnertime was imminent.

"I'll have to look a bit further to find something for you." Somehow Pierce kept his eyes on her face, which wasn't hard to do at all. Her hair was beginning to dry around the edges and it coiled beguilingly along her cheek. And, God, did she have a kissable mouth. His insides were groaning.

Alicia shifted from one bare foot to the other. "I'll dry out in a minute. Don't bother." Despite his resolution, his eyes drifted downward. "Maybe we'd better get them fed," she said hurriedly, and pushed past him. The boys were already sitting at the table where four places had been set. There was a basket of saltines and a tray of sliced cheese and apples in its center. A pan of chili was steaming on the portable butane stove.

She carried the bowls to the table as Pierce ladled them up. Then he held her chair for her before she sat down. Her stomach rumbled rebelliously and he laughed. "I guess the boys aren't the only ones who are hungry."

Good-naturedly she smiled. "I didn't have a chance to eat today."

"She always says that," David piped up. "She doesn't eat breakfast or lunch because she's afraid she'll get fat."

"Yeah," Adam said after cramming his mouth full of crackers, "she exercises every morning with the girl on the television. She gets on the floor and stretches and grunts and her face looks like this." He made a grimace that made Pierce laugh and made Alicia want to kill her second-born.

"Eat your supper so we can get back to our own cabin," she said in typical motherly fashion.

"Can't we stay here?" David whined.

She looked at him with the unmistakable, but silent, parental threat of annihilation. "No, David. We can't intrude on Mr. Reynolds."

"You don't mind, do you?" Adam asked him candidly.

Pierce looked at Alicia across the table. "No, I don't mind. As a matter of fact, I was thinking that I could run back down there and leave a note for your husband. He could join you here when he arrived."

"Husband?" David's young face screwed up in puzzlement.

Alicia's heart stopped and she momentarily closed her eyes. When she had told the lie, it was in the hope of protecting herself and her sons. The boys hadn't heard her. She had never thought the fib would come back to haunt her.

"Your mom told me that your dad is going to meet you at your cabin tonight."

"We don't have a dad," David informed him. "He died."

Adam swallowed his food. "Just like our goldfish. Except Daddy's grave is in the c'metery instead of the backyard."

Alicia felt the green eyes slicing toward her before she even looked up to meet their inquiring gaze. With what defiance she could muster, she met their stare levelly.

"He died a long time ago," David said conversationally. "I remember him but Adam doesn't."

"I do too!" Adam protested. "He had black hair and brown eyes like us.'

"You've just seen pictures of him so you think you remember."

"I remember. Mommy, make David stop saying I don't remember."

While this argument was carried out, the green eyes hadn't released their captive. "I'm sure you remember your daddy, Adam," Pierce said quietly.

"He was big like you, except maybe you're bigger," David continued. "We thought Carter was going to be our new dad, but then he married Sloan instead of Mom."

Alicia's warning glances did nothing to stop the flow of words from the mouths of her babes. "David, I'm sure Mr. Reynolds—"

"I cried when Carter told us he wasn't going to be our dad," Adam expounded. "But Mom said it was okay because Sloan was our friend and we'd get to see Carter a lot and just because he didn't marry her that didn't mean he didn't still love us. Can I have some more chili, please?"

"We can still go to Carter's beach house to play. It's neat. Adam's a pig. He always wants seconds."

"Am not."

"Are too."

Alicia was able to avoid Pierce's questioning eyes as he got up to refill Adam's bowl. He would think she was a complete idiot for fabricating a husband.

"Do you have a dad?" David asked of Pierce as he sat back down.

"No. He died a long time ago. But my mother is still alive."

"You're just like us."

Pierce smiled. "I guess I am."

"Do you have a wife?"

"Adam!" Alicia admonished, ready to throttle both her talkative offspring in one fell swoop. "That's enough. Both of you stop talking and eat your supper."

"No, I don't have a wife." Pierce's eyes were laughing as he blotted his mouth with a napkin.

They finished the meal in what was to Alicia blissful silence. Finally Pierce spoke. "If you're finished, I think it's time to get you two boys to bed." He stood and began to clear the table.

Alicia panicked. "David, Adam, go in the bathroom and wash your hands."

"Do you want us to wash our hands or are you just sending us in there because you want to talk about something you don't want us to hear?"

"Go!" she said, pointing a commanding finger toward the door.

"All right," her precocious son mumbled, taking his younger brother by the hand.

When they had the water running in the bathroom, Alicia whirled on the man. She had to tilt her head back at a drastic angle to look up into his face. Until then she hadn't noticed how tall he was. Or was he just standing closer? "I'm taking my boys back to our cabin. We will not spend the night here and I would appreciate it if you'd stop trying to lure them into staying, thereby making me the villain."

"That's lunacy, Mrs.— Oh, hell. What's your name?"

"Mrs. Russell," she said peevishly. He glared and she relented. "Alicia."

His lips drew up in a quick smile, then thinned to a resolute line. "The rain hasn't slacked off. What possible advantage could it be to drag those two little boys back through the woods to that damp, dark cabin when they could sleep here?"

"Because I'd be sleeping here too."

He shrugged. "So?"

"*So?* So my mother taught me to have better sense than to spend the night with strange men."

"I'm not strange." Again that quick smile, then tight-lipped sternness. "Why did you make up that lie about a husband? To protect yourself from me?"

She tossed back her hair and raised her chin. "Yes. I was hoping you wouldn't bother us if you thought I had a man joining us soon."

Was it only her imagination or did he lean forward slightly and did his voice lower in volume and pitch. "Am I bothering you?"

*Damn right.* That's what she would have had to say if placed under oath. Thankfully she wasn't. "I just think that for all concerned, it would be best if we returned to our cabin."

"I disagree. You'd be alone without power. It's cold out

now and the boys aren't dressed properly, to say nothing of you."

To make his point, his eyes scaled down her bare legs. But something happened on their return trip up to her face. They softened. Dangerously so. So that when they collided with Alicia's, he and she were both rendered speechless by that nonphysical collision. Seconds ticked by, moments stretched out, and still they stared, powerless either to move or look away.

*What is wrong with me?* Alicia asked herself. She had taken this week off to weigh an important decision, a decision she was being pressed for. Her time was running out; they wanted an answer. She didn't need this kind of romantic distraction in her life. Not ever, but particularly not now when she had just found her footing in the scheme of things.

Similar thoughts were parading through Pierce's mind. A week ago, he would have been highly amused by this situation. He would have given his arousal free rein and not battled to suppress it. Wryly he admitted that he would have used any tactic necessary to get this woman into bed with him. But the day before yesterday, his world had been turned upside down and he didn't know how he was going to cope. His problem was solely his. He certainly couldn't invite anyone to share it. And what he had in mind every time he looked at this woman was sharing of the most intimate kind.

"Where's my bed?" Adam's question was rolled out around a broad yawn.

Alicia and Pierce both jumped reflexively and moved apart.

She floundered helplessly. If she refused to stay now that would be tantamount to an admission that Pierce Reynolds *did* bother her. Purely from a logical standpoint, staying in his cabin was the safest, most reasonable thing to do. She would look like a sap traipsing back through the woods during this thunderstorm with her two weary, cranky children in tow.

This would be a temporary relapse, she assured herself. It had taken her thirty-one years to learn to take care of herself. She never wanted to depend on anyone else ever again. But this was only for one night.

Pierce Reynolds's gray-flecked eyebrow arched in query and she answered with a silent lowering of her eyes. He accepted her decision graciously and without a trace of smugness. "I thought one of you boys could sleep down here with me and the other upstairs with your mom. There are twin beds up there."

"They can both sleep upstairs. I wouldn't want you to be crowded." *He would crowd any bed.*

"No problem." *I'd love to be crowded in a bed with you.*

"Then Adam can sleep with you since he's the smaller."

David's brow wrinkled as he eyed his brother jealously. Then he bounded up the stairs. "Goody, I get to sleep upstairs."

They were soon bedded down and the cabin became awkwardly quiet save for the steady cadence of rainfall and the distant rumble of thunder. The worst of the storm had been spent. Alicia began clearing the table, washing the dishes in the sink. Pierce dried and replaced them in the limited cabinet space. They worked in silence until the job was done.

"Thank you," he said.

"It's the least I could do."

"I guess I'd better find you something else to put on. Whether you want to admit it or not, I know those damp clothes are uncomfortable. Mine are."

She wished he hadn't mentioned that. His damp shirt was molded over the muscles of his arms and chest. Tight denim jeans hugged his hips and thighs like a second skin. His bare feet hinted at an intimacy she would rather not think about.

She was thinking about it just the same.

He knelt in front of a cedar bureau and began rifling through the drawers. He had searched two, found them lacking, and closed them before he pulled open the third. His hands plowed through the garments left behind and long forgotten. The drawer produced a stocking cap, one glove, a pair of plaid bermuda shorts about a size forty-two, and three socks all of different colors.

"Ah, here's something." He pulled the garment out of the drawer, eyeing it knowingly. "Someone had a good time while he was here."

Alicia's breath stopped in her throat when he held up a slinky nightgown. Firelight shone through its black transparency. Filaments of fabric formed the shoulder straps. The lace bodice was as fine and fragile as a spider's web. On a human body, it would be no more substantial than smoke, a shadow worn for clothing.

Coming slowly to his feet, he advanced toward her, his eyes immobilizing. He laid the straps of the nightgown against her shoulders, pulled the scanty bodice into place over her breasts, and let the length of it float down over her bare legs to her feet.

He peered at her through the shimmering folds. "Perfect fit," he said in a rough, unnatural voice.

Alicia stood stock still, not daring to move. Feeling vulnerable and much like a succulent dessert about to be devoured, she quavered, "I can't wear this."

To her relief, he stepped back quickly. He looked as though he had suddenly remembered something and whatever it was had yanked him out of a golden fantasy and plunged him into cold reality. His face went blank. His mood changed abuptly. It was so extreme a mood shift that even Alicia, a stranger to him, saw it, felt it. It was tangible.

Maybe he *was* married.

He turned his back, angrily shoved the nightgown out of sight into the drawer, and began to pillage it again. He seemed unaccountably aggravated as he stood up and thrust a man's shirt at her. "You can wear this," he said brusquely. "Good night, Alicia."

# Two

She awoke stretching contentedly. Staring up at the unfamiliar ceiling, it took her a few moments to determine where she was. Then she remembered.

Sitting bolt upright, she tossed the covers back. The other bed was empty. When she had climbed the narrow stairs the night before, she hadn't thought she would sleep so deeply or so long. One glance out the small window in the atticlike loft told her that the sun was well up on a gorgeous fall day. The woods seemed to have been washed clean by the storm.

A high-pitched giggle followed by a chorus of "Shhhh" came from downstairs. Alicia tiptoed to the top of the stairs and listened. She heard the clatter of silverware against dishes and smelled the wonderful aromas of bacon and maple syrup and coffee.

"Keep your voices down and let your mother sleep. She was very tired last night."

"Can I have some more pancakes?"

"Sure, Adam. How many does that make?" There was laughter in the deep, husky voice.

"Don't know."

"About sixty," David said, and Alicia could tell that despite her lectures he was talking with his mouth full. "I told you he's a pig."

"So are you!"

"Hey, cool it, both of you. Here, David, here's two more for you too."

"You make good pancakes."

"Thanks, Adam."

"Not quite as good as Mom's though," he said loyally.

From her hidden perch Alicia smiled. She heard Pierce's laugh and it caused a fluttering in the pit of her stomach. Her clothes had been carefully draped over the end rail of the iron bed, but they were still damp. The thought of pulling them on was repugnant. Tugging self-consciously on the hem of the man's shirt, she took the first few stairs down.

"Good morning," she said tentatively.

Three heads turned in her direction. Two spoke, one remained silent. "Hi, Mom." "Pierce fixed us pancakes and bacon." "Watch it, Pierce, you're dripping the batter on the floor."

Pierce looked properly abashed and dropped the spoon back into the large mixing bowl. He had been so taken by the sight of Alicia's legs, the soft way the shirt clung to her breasts before falling mid-thigh, the tousled blond hair wreathing her head, and the sleepy-warm flush of her complexion that he had been momentarily dumbfounded.

Alicia knew she must look like the very devil. Her makeup was now almost twenty-four hours old. Every time she moved her face it seemed to crack and she could feel loose flakes of mascara precariously clinging to her lashes. Her hair had been rained on and she didn't even have a brush with her. Knowing that a wrong move could reveal more of her thighs than needed to be revealed, she descended the staircase with stiff carefulness.

She patted each son on the head. "How early did you get Mr. Reynolds up?"

"He was already up. He jogs every morning," David provided.

"Would you like a cup of coffee?"

Having run out of things to do to avoid it, she glanced up at her host. His cheeks were ruddy, as though he'd been outdoors and kissed by an early morning mountain chill. The ash-silver hair was agreeably mussed, falling softly on the tops of his ears and shirt collar. The green eyes were as startling now as they had been the night before. He smelled of clean air, a recent shower, and a woodsy fragrance.

"Yes, please," Alicia said. Her voice had very little power behind it and came out a breathy gust that she hoped he wouldn't take the wrong way.

He poured her a cup of coffee, pointing out the cream and sugar on the table. "Have a seat and I'll grill you a stack of pancakes."

"No, thank you."

"See I told you. All she thinks about is getting fat."

"David Russell . . ." Alicia shook a warning finger at him and both boys collapsed into a fit of giggles.

Pierce was laughing too. "Everybody has to eat breakfast in the mountains. Besides, I haven't eaten yet. I was waiting for you. It would be unfair to make me eat alone."

Alicia sighed her consent and Pierce poured disks of batter onto the hot grill. "Since you boys are finished, why don't you go make the beds while your Mom and I are eating? I don't want to see one wrinkle in the covers when you're done."

"Yes, sir," they said in unison and nearly ran over

each other scrambling up the stairs. Alicia watched their enthusiastic retreat in wonder.

"How did you do that?"

"What?"

"Get them to make the beds without a fuss."

He grinned as he flipped three perfect golden circular pancakes onto her plate. "It's different when someone besides Mom asks you to do something."

"I guess you're right," she said, liberally and sinfully buttering the pancakes. Her mouth was watering. She was just as generous with the syrup.

"Bacon?"

"Two please."

"More coffee?"

"Yes."

By the time he swung a long jean-clad leg over the back of his chair and joined her, she was well into the stack of pancakes. "These are delicious."

"Thanks." He smiled his pleasure as he watched her eat. "The power came back on sometime during the night, so I was able to use the grill. Otherwise the menu might have been boiled eggs."

She laid her fork down, realizing for the first time that the electricity had indeed been restored. Why hadn't she noticed something that important before? Was it because this cabin was so comfortable that she subconsciously dreaded returning to her own and leaving the company of this man?

"Good," she said, taking a sip of coffee with an assumed air of nonchalance. Something in the way he looked at her across the breakfast table made her uncomfortably aware of her bare thighs on the seat of the chair and that only a pair of panties kept her from being naked beneath the shirt.

She felt very naked.

"We'll have to get to our cabin and out of your way as soon as I help with the dishes."

"How did your husband die?"

The question was so out of context that Alicia felt it like a well-placed sock to her jaw. Slightly stunned, she looked at Pierce. He had finished eating and was holding his coffee cup high, just under his chin, with both hands. He stared at her through the steam that rose from it.

She saw no reason not to answer him, even though it was an impertinent question for one stranger to ask of another. "He was a businessman, but his avocation was racing sports cars. One Sunday afternoon, he was racing and . . ." She lowered her eyes to her ravaged plate. "He had an accident. He died instantly."

Pierce set his cup down and folded his arms on the tabletop, leaning forward slightly. She got the distinct impression that he wanted to touch her, to offer condolence. "You couldn't have been married long."

Alicia's smile was wistful. "Long enough to have David and Adam barely two years apart. We married while still in college. I fell in love with Jim Russell the first time I saw him."

Pierce was alarmed by the jealousy that took a stranglehold on him. He was also swamped by a feeling of supreme frustration. *Why now?* Why now was he meeting a lovely woman who exuded a latent sexuality longing to be released? A woman who happened to be an unfairly young widow.

When that internal anger seized him again, Alicia was aware of it. His face changed, becoming hard and closed. Anxiety pinched the corners of his eyes and mouth. Pierce Reynolds was a man with an ax to grind. The sooner she was away from him, the better.

"We should get started," she said uneasily. She didn't

need a man in her life. Not now. Not anymore. And she especially didn't need one with problems.

Briskly she set about cleaning the kitchen. Once upstairs, she pulled on her sour smelling clothes and hustled the boys out of their UCLA T-shirts and back into their own shirts and shorts. She disregarded their litany of protests and querulous questions.

"I can't tell you how much I appreciate your kindness and hospitality, Mr. Reynolds." God, she sounded like a paragraph out of an etiquette handbook and felt just a little ridiculous standing in the cut-offs when it was too cold for them. Her tennis shoes were like clammy weights tied onto her feet. The small group was gathered on the porch of the cabin.

"I'm glad I was here to help." Pierce's tone was just as detached and formal. "You're sure you'll be all right?"

"Yes. Thank you again."

The two boys looked about as jolly as pallbearers. Pierce knelt down in front of them. He gave each of them a quarter. "Play a game of Pac Man for me the next chance you get."

When they continued to hang their heads in glum silence, Alicia prodded. "What do you say?"

"Thank you," they mumbled. David lifted his head. "Did you ever play soccer, Pierce?"

"Football."

"No kidding? Which position?"

"Halfback."

"Gee. A running back. I'm too young to play football, but I'm a forward on my soccer team. We're the Hurricanes."

"I'll bet you're a good forward."

The dark eyes lit up. "Maybe you could come see me play sometime."

Alicia's heart wrenched at the pitiful plea in the young voice. David desperately needed a masculine role model.

But she had learned long ago she couldn't simply provide her children with a father. She would be taking on a husband too. Since she and Carter had broken their engagement, there had been no serious candidates for that.

"Maybe sometime." But he knew he wouldn't. He couldn't.

"Where is your house?" Adam asked.

"In Los Angeles."

"That's where our house is too."

"Come on, boys. Say good-bye and thank Mr. Reynolds again," Alicia intervened before their departure stretched out any longer.

"Thanks," they muttered sadly as Alicia all but dragged them across the clearing, past the parked jeep that she hadn't seen the night before, and into the woods that separated the cabins.

"Oh, we're going to have such fun," she said, warding off her own sense of loss and depression. "Just wait and see. Maybe after we get settled, we'll go fishing."

"You won't want to bait the hooks," David grumbled.

He was right. The whole idea made her queasy. But she had had to do worse. "Wanna bet? You can show me how."

Her forced enthusiasm lasted as long as their walk through the woods and past the front door of the cabin. Then the three of them came to an abrupt standstill and gazed about them in mute disbelief. The cabin was a wreck.

A tree limb, driven by the wind, had torn through a screen and crashed through a window, leaving the floor and one bed showered with glass. Heavy rain had blown in. The floor was puddled in several places. The beds and even the one sofa were saturated. The curtains hung on the window in soggy tatters. Alicia reached for the light switch. Nothing happened. The electricity may have been restored in Pierce's cabin, but not here.

She shivered to think what would have happened had they not joined Pierce last night. What if one of them had been lying on that bed when the limb crashed through the window? They had escaped possible injury and for that she would be eternally grateful. But what was she going to do now? Were it not for her boys, she would have sat down and cried.

To her dismay, her sons were jubilant. "Can we go back to Pierce's cabin?"

"Can we, Mom? We liked it there."

"We'll be good. We promise. Won't we, Adam?"

"We'll be good."

"No," she cried, facing them and immediately dousing their expectations. At their collapsing expressions, she ventured a wide false smile. "Don't be silly. We can't force ourselves on Mr. Reynolds."

"Then what are we gonna do?" David demanded.

"I don't know." If she had let her dejection show, she would have sunk to the floor and curled into a tight ball. She hated being solely responsible all the time, having to provide all the answers, make all the decisions. But wasn't that what she had set out to prove after Carter had married Sloan, that she *could* and *would* be responsible for her own life and that of her sons?

She had survived the sudden death of a husband, a broken engagement, she had landed herself a peach of a job that she loved and was good at. By God, she wasn't going to let these setbacks ruin their vacation!

She clapped her hands together. "The first thing we're going to do is change clothes. It's much cooler here than it was in the valley, so David, Adam, help me carry in our luggage."

Despondently they obeyed, but they seemed to revive when they were dressed in jeans and long sleeved

T-shirts. After a cold hasty shower and shampoo in the small bathroom, Alicia pulled on an old pair of jeans and a sweatshirt left over from college days. It was still splattered with the paint she and Sloan had used to redecorate their room in the sorority house.

"Well, it's for certain we can't stay here," Alicia said, assessing the damage in the main room of the cabin. "We'll drive down to the lodge. They have cabins that they rent out by the week. We'll see if one is available."

"What if there isn't?"

*What if there isn't?* "Then we'll go somewhere else," she said with more bright cheerfulness than she felt. "Let's get the bags back in the car." She checked the ice chest she had brought along. Most of the ice had melted. If she didn't refrigerate the groceries soon, she'd have to throw them away. But that was the least of her problems.

First priority was to find them lodging, someplace where the boys could fish and hike and generally soak up Mother Nature, which she had been promising to let them do for months. Not too isolated, not too crowded, not too far from home. Woods, mountain air. This place had been perfect. Now she might have to take what she could find. Rescheduling the trip would cause innumerable problems. She had arranged with the boys' teachers to excuse them this week. Undoing all that would be a pain.

The clerk at the main desk of the lodge listened sympathetically when she told him about the storm damage the cabin had sustained.

He scratched behind his ear. "Course, those places up there on that ridge are privately owned."

"I know that, but I've already called my friend who owns it. She gave me permission to see that things are cleaned up and the window repaired. She'll pay the bill. Could you find someone to take care of that for me?"

"Sure, sure. See no problem with that. I can have someone out this afternoon to get started."

"Thank you. Now we need a place to stay. We'd like to rent one of your cabins for the week."

"This week?"

Alicia mentally counted to ten. "Yes, this week. Right now."

He must have had a terrible itch behind his ear, for he was scratching it again. "Don't have any available, little lady."

Alicia clenched her teeth against the chauvinistic slur and instructed Adam to keep his fingers out of the ears of the buffalo head mounted over the mantel of the lodge's fireplace. She tried cajoling. "Surely you have something. I don't care how large or how small—"

"Nothing," he said emphatically, and flipped open a reservation book. "Let's see here. . . . We'll have a cabin that sleeps six on December fifteenth. Not many folks come up here around Christmastime, you see."

When he said nothing, he meant nothing. She spent a half hour plugging the pay telephone with quarters trying to find them an alternate recreation spot within driving distance. She wasted her quarters and her time.

"I'm sorry, but there's nothing I can do." She had a consoling hand on each boy's shoulder. "We'll have to go home and plan another trip."

"That's not fair. You promised!"

"David, I know it doesn't seem fair. I was looking forward to this week off too."

"No, you weren't. You don't care if we have to go home. You didn't want to camp. You're a silly girl. You're *glad* everything's been ruined!"

"Now listen to me, young man—"

The jeep braked just a few feet beyond the porch of the lodge and Pierce stepped out of it. He looked breathtakingly handsome in a plaid flannel shirt with a down vest over it. "What's going on?"

Before Alicia could open her mouth, Adam and David ran toward him spouting a barrage of broken sentences that more or less told him what had happened. Over their heads, he looked at Alicia.

"David," Pierce said, fishing in the tight pocket of his jeans for a dollar bill. "Will you and Adam go into the lodge and buy me a newspaper, please?"

"Come on, Adam," David said wearily. "They're gonna talk grown-up again and don't want us to hear."

As Adam followed his brother through the door, he was heard to say, "Remember when Carter had to talk to Mom grown-up? They made us go away all the time."

Embarrassed, Alicia looked up at Pierce, but he was smiling. "I think they're making kids smarter these days."

She didn't feel much like smiling, but she managed a wobbly one. "I think so too."

"Now, what happened?"

Slowly, and in more coherent detail, she explained what had happened. "They're not reconciled to the fact that this outing wasn't meant to be."

"Wasn't it?"

The soft urgency in his voice brought her head up and she met his eyes. They were hot, burning into hers. She couldn't look at them long and averted her head. "No, I don't think it was. Everything's gone wrong. I'm not the outdoorsy type and they know it. Of course they blame me for this fiasco."

He propped his shoulder against a redwood post that supported the porch's overhang and gazed out over the gravel road and into the dense woods on the other side. He was weighing a decision. She somehow knew this and stood by silently, unable to move away, compelled by some unknown force to wait him out.

He spoke with methodic precision. "Why don't you and the boys stay with me?" He turned to look at her. "In my cabin."

Unconsciously, she twisted her hands together. "We can't."

"Why? Because you know I want to make love to you?"

Four things happened at once. Her eyes rounded. Her face paled considerably. She gasped sharply. Her tongue darted out to wet her lips.

"I'm not a man to mince words, Alicia. Let's be frank. From the first time I saw you in the light, standing dripping wet by the front door, I've wanted you in bed with me. Before that actually, when you were bending over the fuse box. Even when I thought you were another man's wife, I desired you. And you knew it."

"Don't—"

"But I would never do anything about it." Her protests died in her throat from surprise. When he was certain she would hear him out, he continued. "First, you would probably be insulted if I even tried to coax you into my bed. I'd never want to risk offending you." He drew a deep breath and turned away from her again to stare vacantly into the distance. "Secondly, I have reasons not to get involved with anyone right now. Viable, prohibitive reasons. Especially since . . ."

She swallowed. "Since?"

He swiveled around to face her. "Never mind." He smiled. "Knowing that I would never take advantage of you or compromise you in any way, will you consent to sharing the cabin?"

She rubbed her forehead with her thumb and middle finger while she groped for a sound reason not to accept. His invitation was seeming less and less absurd. "I'm not afraid of you. I don't think you're a man of uncontrollable impulses."

He laughed then. "Don't press your luck. I still find

you damnably attractive. If you were to come out in that black nightgown I found last night, all these vows of celibacy would be shot to hell."

She blushed and hurriedly changed the subject. "I can't let us interrupt your vacation. Do you have any idea what the boys can be like when they get wound up?"

"No," he replied solemnly. "I missed parenting altogether. But I'd love to know what it's like. Your boys are a delight and I'm already looking forward to having them underfoot."

She shook her head in bewilderment, unaware that the gesture made the sunlight shimmer in her hair. It was all Pierce could do to keep his hands out of it. "I don't think you know what you're letting yourself in for."

"Let me worry about that." He took a step forward, not too close, but close enough to smell her morning cologne, close enough to feel her body heat. "Please say you'll stay. I want you to."

Throat arched, head thrown back, she peered up into his face, trying to decide if she had heard a trace of quiet desperation in his entreaty or if she were imagining it. How old was he? Early forties? His face had the firm stamp of mature masculinity on it, but wasn't coarse. His brows were thick and often spoke eloquently for themselves. A finely sculpted nose, long and narrow and slightly flared at the nostrils, went well with a full and sensuous lower lip. Looking at his mouth made her think shamefully erotic thoughts.

For that reason alone she should refuse his invitation. There were many reasons not to accept. Capsulizing them, it was just plain stupid and highly irresponsible to spend a week with a total stranger. Despite his manners and cultured voice and obvious intelligence, she knew nothing about him beyond his name and that he had a living mother and no wife. But instinctively she trusted him. She chose to trust her instincts. "Are you sure?"

His answer was a broad grin. Just then the boys came bounding out the door of the lodge with Pierce's newspaper. He scooped Adam up in his arms, straining biceps Alicia couldn't help but be impressed by. "Guess what, fellows. You're going to stay with me this week. So the only place you're going now is to help me unload your car at my cabin."

They whooped with noisy glee. "Can we ride in the jeep? We've never ridden in a jeep before."

Pierce laid a hand on David's shoulder. "Yes, you may ride in the jeep, but first you have an apology to make to your mother, don't you?"

Both Alicia and David looked up at him in bewilderment. "What for?" David asked.

"I heard your tone of voice and what you said to her when I drove up. You were blaming her for something that was beyond her control. Do you think that's fair?"

David's chin fell almost to his knees. "No, sir," he mumbled into his chest.

"You're the man of the family. As such, you should know to accept things graciously when there's nothing you can do to change them. Don't you think so?"

"Yes, sir." The boy turned to his mother. "I'm sorry."

Alicia knelt down and hugged him hard. "Apology accepted. Now let's concentrate on having a good time, all right?"

David smiled tremulously. Pierce curved his hand around the back of the boy's neck and steered him toward the jeep. "Why don't you sit in the front seat this time and help me navigate?"

"Can I too, Pierce?" Adam wanted to know as he trotted after them on his chubby legs.

"Next time." He glanced over his shoulder to see Alicia

standing where they had left her. "Coming?" he asked softly.

She nodded. "I need to make arrangements for the repairs on the cabin with the clerk. I'll follow in our car." As she watched them go, she wondered why there were tears in her eyes.

The day didn't lack for activity. It was a chore to unload her car and find a place for everything in the cabin. Then Pierce took the boys on a wood gathering mission while Alicia prepared a lunch of soup and sandwiches. In the afternoon they hiked around the lake, and returned to cook steaks on the outdoor barbecue someone had had the foresight to build when the cabin was constructed. The dinner was sumptuous, but the boys yawned through theirs. Immediately afterward they were bathed and put to bed.

Alicia went to sit on the front steps of the cabin, to soak up the silence, the crisp night air, the star-studded sky undimmed by city lights. Pierce joined her, carrying two mugs of coffee, one of which she accepted with a soft thank you. Rather than being an intrusion, she found that his presence enhanced her sense of peacefulness.

"They're already asleep."

"I hope Adam's snoring doesn't keep you awake."

"I've been told I snore too."

Alicia wondered how many women had told him that. To keep her mind from wandering in that direction, she guided it to neutral territory. "You said your company owns the cabin. What company?"

"Ecto Engineers."

"What kind of engineering?"

"Aeronautical."

"You design airplanes? Military planes? What?"

He settled and she liked the sound and feel of his male

body shifting comfortably. "We do some military contracts. Mostly we work with private aircraft firms, design corporate jets, that kind of thing."

"Are your designs brilliant and innovative?" She was teasing.

"Yes," he answered honestly and smiled a dashing smile. They both laughed softly.

She glanced over her shoulder toward the dark cabin. "What would the owners of your company say if they knew you had invited a widow and her brood to share their cabin with you?"

"Well, since I'm a full partner in the company, I'm entitled to invite whomever I want." She might have guessed that he wasn't a wage earner. He reeked of success. Even his casual clothes bespoke good taste that one paid a high price for.

"What about you?" he asked. "What work do you do?"

"I'm an assistant fashion coordinator for three boutiques. Glad Rags we're called." His eyes took in her ponytail, paint-smeared sweatshirt, jeans, and sneakers. She laughed. "You're too polite to make a sarcastic comment." Her elbow found his ribs and because he was as warm as a stove, she didn't move away as quickly as she should have.

"I'm the epitome of diplomacy," he said, wishing she hadn't moved away after touching him, even if it was with her elbow. She was so damned soft, so indubitably feminine. "What does an assistant fashion coordinator do?"

"Helps plan the overall fashion statement the stores are going to project for a particular season."

"In plain English, what the hell does that mean?"

She laughed and marveled at how relaxed she was. "For instance, are we going to be trendy or understated? Do we push ensembles or coordinates? Are we going to be avant-garde or classical? Does that make sense?"

"More or less. Do you like it?"

"I love it. I've been preparing for it all my life and didn't know it. Despite what you see here"—she bowed her head mockingly—"I love clothes, have a knack for putting things together, and shopping has always been one of my favorite pastimes. Now I can do it with someone else's money." Her face clouded as she remembered her dilemma.

"What is it?"

"I don't want to burden you with my problems."

"I asked."

Setting her coffee mug aside, she studied him for a moment before she began. It felt good to talk to an adult, someone objective, uninvolved. She had eliminated her parents and good friends, even Sloan and Carter, as able to give her an unbiased opinion.

"My supervisor is expecting a baby next month and has decided to leave for good. It's her cabin I was borrowing," she said as an aside. "Anyway, the owners of the stores have offered me her job. They know a lot about merchandising and money management and absolutely nothing about taste and fashion. I have until the end of the month to give them my answer before they start looking for someone else."

"What will you decide?"

She leaned back, propping herself up with straight arms. If she had realized how that pose emphasized the shape and size of her breasts and the effect it had on Pierce, she wouldn't have sat that way. "I don't know, Pierce." It was the first time she had said his name and swung her head around to see if he had noticed.

"I like that much better than Mr. Reynolds," he said softly. He tugged on a wayward curl before tucking it behind her ear and lamented the multitude of reasons why he couldn't smooth his palm over her breast and seek the nipple with his thumb. "Do you want the job?"

"Yes. It's challenging and exciting. I'd make much more money."

"Well then?"

"It's a demanding job that requires long hours and some travel. I worry about short-changing the boys as it is. They have only one parent. Don't I owe them my undivided attention? I feel guilty if I'm five minutes late getting home."

"You owe something to yourself too. Adam and David will be on their own one day. If you've devoted your life exclusively to them, where will that leave you?"

"I've thought of all that," she said slowly. She had argued with herself until she was blue in the face and the solution to her dilemma still eluded her. Her time was running out. She must make a decision.

But not tonight.

"Thanks for being a sounding board."

"My pleasure." He took her hand. "You'll make the right choice, Alicia."

It was a long time before she could find the will to pull her hand from the warm strength of his. She knew being held in his arms would feel even better. They would be even warmer, stronger. "I think I'd better go upstairs now."

"Who is Carter?"

# *Three*

His question caught her hunched and ready to stand up, but brought her bottom back down onto the wooden porch with a jolt. "Why do you ask?"

"Because the boys refer to him constantly. Carter said, Carter did. Just about everything in their world is measured by how Carter would respond to it. I'm curious."

"Carter Madison." She knew full well it wasn't strictly curiosity that had caused him to ask. His face was too tense for mild curiosity. "He's an old friend."

"Carter Madison, Carter Madison." Pierce repeated the name like rapidly snapping fingers. He was trying to place it and when he did, he turned to her. "Carter Madison the writer?"

"You've heard of him. He'd like that."

"I've read most of his novels."

"He'd like that even better."

"I've seen him interviewed on television talk shows. Charming, glib, good-looking guy. What happened? Why didn't you marry him?"

So, he remembered the tale the boys had told him the night before. No wonder he was inquisitive. "He married my best friend, Sloan, instead." Pierce's face went blank, as though he thought he had committed an unpardonable blunder. Alicia relieved his mind by explaining. "Carter was my husband Jim's best friend. After Jim was killed, Carter was marvelous. He felt responsible for me and sheltered me from some of the most unpleasant aspects of recent widowhood. He helped me with the boys. Eventually he became an essential factor in our lives. I hate to admit it, but we took him for granted. He asked me to marry him and I accepted. I felt lost, lonely. Carter was a familiar, safe bulwark to lean against for protection."

She smiled with fond memories. Husbands and wives should be good friends, but good friends should never become husband and wife. "I sent Carter to Sloan's bed and breakfast house in San Francisco so he could finish a book before the wedding. They were instantly attracted to one another. It didn't take him long to realize that he was marrying me for the wrong reasons. Almost simultaneously I realized the same thing. We broke off the engagement the day of the wedding and he married Sloan a few weeks later. They're very happy. She's expecting their first child."

Pierce sipped his coffee, which had to be cold by now. Alicia thought he did it more for something to do to cover his unwarranted interest than because he wanted the coffee. "No regrets?"

"Absolutely none. I love Carter. I always did, as Jim's and my friend. I love Sloan, who remains my best friend. I'm very glad to have been instrumental in bringing them together. They needed each other."

"There's been no one else in your life since Jim's death?"

"No."

She had tried the singles scene for a while, but found that kind of life wasn't for her. Before she and Carter had acknowledged what a mistake they were making, there had been a skiing weekend in Tahoe. A friend, who was much more accustomed to the singles life than Alicia, had enticed her to go. She had had a good time, met a very nice man named Mac, and ended up staying the night in his room. It had felt good to be held, to be loved. Her relationship with Carter had never gone far beyond the platonic. Mac's affection had been just what she needed at the time.

But later, when he had come down from his home in Oregon to see her, he was still nice, he was still attentive and affectionate, but the magic of having a weekend fling in Tahoe was missing. They had endured a strained dinner together and he had said good night at her door, both of them chagrined and a little sad that it hadn't been the same. He hadn't pressed the issue or tried to force anything. She had appreciated that and was glad that he didn't call again.

Well-meaning friends, erroneously under the impression that she was grieving over her loss of Carter, paired her with any number of eligible men. Most of those evenings had been disasters and it was a relief to both her and her escort when they were over.

She had frequented the singles bars and discos with girlfriends who were currently unattached. They hovered like circling vultures waiting for an available man to drop before swooping down on him. The whole scene seemed tawdry and sleazy and Alicia felt cheapened by it. She started making excuses not to go until they stopped calling to invite her. The well of her social life dried up about the time she found her job and after that she didn't miss it.

Only now, in retrospect, did she realize how she had missed talking to an adult. A man. *That's a euphe-*

*mism, Alicia. What you've missed is the scent and strength of masculinity. And admit it, it feels good having this man near you.*

She missed something else too. But she couldn't allow herself to think about that. The love she and Jim had shared in their marriage bed had been so special, she never wanted to settle for anything less. Still, Pierce was extremely attractive and she felt that just beneath his veneer of polished manners, sexuality seethed like a cauldron ready to boil over. What kind of lover would he be? Tender and relaxed or fierce and intense? Or an exciting combination?

She yanked herself out of her musings and stood up quickly. "Well, good night."

"Good night. Don't forget the fishing trip first thing in the morning."

She groaned. "David and Adam were ecstatic about the fishing boat, but I'm concerned. They've never been on a lake in such a small boat. Do you think it's safe?"

"We'll lay down the maritime rules and regulations before we even embark." He saluted and she laughed.

"I know I sound like a mother."

"You sound like a sensible, caring, loving woman."

The way he said it made her throat go dry. There was no moisture with which to wet her lower lip when she dragged her tongue along it.

"Alicia, are you glad you stayed?" Shadows kept her from seeing his face, which was just as well. Longing and desire were nakedly apparent.

"Yes." She tried to sound cheerful and bright and peppy. She sounded breathless and aroused and languorous.

"Good," he said, nodding slowly. "Good."

In vain, she tried to wet her lips again. "Are you coming in? Shall I turn off the lights?"

He shook his head. "No. I'll be in shortly."

The screen door closed behind her and he heard her soft tread on the stairs to the sleeping loft. He could still smell her hair, still see her eyes reflecting the moonlight, creating twin clusters of sapphires and diamonds beneath perfectly arched brows, still detail the shapely swell of her breasts.

He didn't follow her in because he knew if he did, he couldn't have stopped himself from taking her in his arms, pressing her softness against him, kissing her deeply and without restraint, touching her, tasting her, and making her his.

Alicia awoke from her second night under Pierce's roof the same way she had the previous morning, well rested and with a feeling of contentment. Stretching luxuriously, she glanced at the other twin bed, and, as on the first morning, David had already left it. Lazily, she indulged herself and lay still for a moment, enjoying the concert of the birds in the trees outside.

It came to her suddenly that that was the only sound she heard. This morning there was no commotion in the kitchen. The boys were being awfully quiet in light of the fact that they were going fishing.

Alicia threw back the covers and padded to the stairs on bare feet. She had slept in her own nightgown last night, but it covered little more than the borrowed shirt had despite the fact that it came to her ankles. Its scooped neckline showed an expanse of creamy California-tanned décolletage. The sleeveless bodice left her arms bare.

She tripped down the stairs, becoming more panicked with each step. There was no movement in the house. It was sleepy and quiet. Maybe they had gotten up and gone without her, but she doubted Pierce would leave her to worry like this. She ran toward the front door which was standing slightly ajar, pulled it open, and scanned the grounds surrounding the cabin. Nothing. Yes, they had probably gone without her.

Just then she heard rustling movements behind her and whirled around. My God! Pierce was sound asleep, alone in the double bed. Alicia's heart began to pound out danger signals. She gave the forebodingly empty cabin one more hasty inspection before she crammed her fingers against her mouth to stifle a whimper of panic, at the same time bolting for the bed.

"Pierce!" The heel of her hand landed hard on his shoulder with the impetus of her lunge behind it.

"What?" His eyes popped open wildly as he struggled to sit up. He shook his head to clear it. "What?"

"The boys are gone." The words were clipped, emphatic, rapid, like bullets being fired from the barrel of a gun.

He stared at her blankly for a moment. Didn't he remember her, recognize her? "The boys are gone?" he repeated.

Her head bobbed in frantic confirmation. "I don't see them anywhere outside. They're gone." Her voice cracked on the last word, and that seemed to finally alert Pierce to her distress. The covers were flung back and he sprang off the bed.

His hands closed around her shoulders. "They're okay. I'm sure of it. They probably just wandered off." His palms were moving up and down her arms, warming her, the way a paramedic would try to revive a victim of shock. "Maybe they're on their way down to the boat."

"At the lake? Oh, God. They won't know the danger. What if they try to get in the boat?"

He pulled her to him quickly, hard, crushing her against his body and pressing her face into his chest. "It's all right. I promise it is." He whispered urgently into her hair, willing her to believe him. "Hurry now. Let's dress and go look." He pushed her away and peered into her eyes.

She nodded mechanically and turned to run up the stairs, catching her nightgown in a damp fist and hiking it high. In minutes they met at the front door. "They were so excited about the fishing, I think the pier is our best bet to start," Pierce told her as they scrambled down the steps of the porch.

"So do I." Even the pinkish golden rays of the new morning sun didn't relieve the pallor of her face.

Pierce took her hand and they ran down the overgrown path that led from the cabin toward the lake. He did his best to push aside tree limbs and warn her of roots that snaked across the trail, but she stumbled along behind him, fear and dread making her blind to the hazards. By the time the lake came into sight like a silver platter lying amidst the woods, she had been scratched and bruised.

"Do you see them?" Anxiously she stepped around Pierce where he had halted on the edge of the clearing.

"Yes," he said, letting out the word on a long exhalation. Alicia knew then that he had been just as concerned as she, but had remained calm for her benefit. He pointed in the direction of the pier. Both boys were sitting on it, legs dangling over the water. They were happily chatting, blissfully unaware of the chaos they had caused in their mother's heart.

Pierce took her hand and they jogged down the gradual slope to the pier. The boys heard them coming and ran to meet them. "We're gonna catch millions of fish. We've been watching them, haven't we, Adam?"

"They swim right up to the pier."

The two young faces turned up to the adults were flushed with excitement and high color. "Are you ready? The poles are in the boat. Adam and me checked."

Alicia paled again to think of them climbing in and

out of the boat that was moored at the water's edge. They had taken swimming lessons for the last three summers and both could swim fairly well. But a neighborhood pool where the depth of the water was clearly demarcated and the cold, murky waters of a lake were two different things entirely. "David, Adam, I was scared out of my wits!"

For the first time the boys realized that their mother and Pierce weren't smiling and their exuberance was immediately snuffed out. Their smiles deflated and they took steps backward, away from the wrath they felt coming.

"It was extremely dangerous for the two of you to come down here alone." Pierce's brows were as scolding as his tone of voice.

"We didn't do anything wrong, honest, Pierce," David said in a small voice.

"You left the cabin without permission. That was very wrong. Your mother woke up and you weren't there. She was worried half to death and so was I."

David and Adam looked mournfully at each other. Adam's lip began to quiver. "David wanted to get to the lake early."

"So did you!" David said, wheeling on his brother. "He came upstairs and woke me up. He—"

"It doesn't matter whose idea it was," Alicia said with forced calm. Now that she knew they were all right, she was trembling on the inside from the aftershocks that still assailed her. "Don't ever, *ever* wander off like that without letting me know where you are."

"Are we in trouble?"

"Can we still go fishing?"

"Did you understand what your mother said?" Pierce's voice was so intimidating that even Alicia flinched. "You are never to disappear like that again." Both boys hung their heads in contrition and answered with meek "yes, sirs." They were miserable, but Pierce didn't relent. "Let's go back to the cabin. We want a cup of coffee and I think you should eat some breakfast before we get started."

"Then we still get to go?" David asked, bravely, hopefully.

Now that they seemed to have learned their lesson, it was all Pierce could do to keep from smiling. "Alicia and I will talk about it on the way back. It might make a difference if, when we get back, we find the beds being made and the cabin straightened."

David streaked off toward the trail, Adam doing his best to keep up with him.

Alicia slumped as the tension eked out of her. She gazed at her sons, realizing, as parents are wont to do after a crisis, just how tenuous their lives were and how important they were to her. "Thank you." Her voice was husky with emotion. "I was ready to light into them out of fear and anger. You handled it perfectly by properly chastising them but also making sure they understood their mistake."

He laughed shortly. "They're not my kids. That makes it a helluva lot simpler."

"But you were worried too."

"I was worried too," he admitted ruefully. He touched her arm. "You okay?"

She shuddered briefly to shake off the last traces of trauma and looked up at him. "Yes, I'm fine now."

Their eyes melted together. Realization of what had happened only minutes ago dawned on them at the same time. It had had a stunning impact on them, but they hadn't been able to pause and dwell on it then. The indulgence had been postponed until now, now when they could afford the time, could devote to it the concentration such an occurrence deserved.

Her mind tracked backward and Alicia could see him

coming off the bed, a study of virile grace and power, naked save for a pair of briefs that hid nothing and emphasized much. There was much to emphasize.

Her palms began to perspire.

The chest hair that matted the hard curves had tickled her nose as he held her tightly against him. He was an even toasty tan color all over. She had longed to explore him slowly, to drink in with the sensors on her palms the varied textures. He had offered her comfort when she needed it, but at the same time he had acquainted her with his rawly masculine body.

Pierce was remembering too. But his recollections were of softness, the kind a man is compelled to cover, to protect, to mate with, the kind of softness hard virility yearns to be nestled in. Blond hair was riotous around her head, much as it was now. It fell on skin the color of ripe peaches and he had longed to taste it. He had wanted to taste her mouth, too, a mouth that seemed in perpetual need of kissing.

Her breasts had swayed lush and heavy and heavenly beneath her nightgown. When she was bending over him, shaking him awake, he had seen their full glory displayed under the gaping neckline of the gown. Almost as enticing were the dusky shadows of her nipples that shyly pushed against the cloudlike cotton when she was standing straight. He remembered what it felt like to hold her against him, to feel the blatant femininity that roused every sleeping cell in his body.

And now it had become just too much to resist. He simply had to kiss her.

One hand cupped her jaw and tilted her face up. The other went inside her jacket. His arm curved dictatorially around her back and hauled her close.

"Pierce—"

His mouth came down on hers, slanting over surprised, slightly parted lips that didn't stand a chance against the onslaught. It was a potent kiss and had an immediacy about it that coerced her lips to relax against the thrusts of his tongue. It was buried in the soft, sweet recess of her mouth where it refused to be stilled and continued its stroking.

Later, Alicia assured herself that she had struggled and that his greater strength had overpowered her. She lied to herself. For actually her body inclined toward his and her feet followed with tiny baby steps that brought them between his hard straddling legs. There was no denying that he wanted her in the most primeval way. He was a steely hard pressure against the fly of her jeans.

But his mouth was softly persuasive. Against such gentle persuasion, she had no argument. His kiss made her feel as if she were the most desirable woman in the world, the only woman in the world, and that if he didn't have her, he might perish.

When at last he lifted his head, he seemed impatient with himself. The hand securing her jaw dropped to his side and the other was withdrawn from her jacket. "We'd better get back and see to the boys," he said gruffly before turning in the direction of the cabin.

Left with a sense of loss, Alicia forlornly followed him. She hadn't invited his kiss. It shouldn't have happened. But since it had, she wished he had cuddled her for a while afterward.

Such romantic sentiments were utter foolishness. She didn't want this man. Did she?

Fishing in the boat turned out to be a complete success. Pierce instructed the boys on what they could and could not do in a boat that small and they returned to the pier with a creel of fish and four slightly sunburned noses.

In the afternoon, Alicia opted for a nap while the "men" went into town for groceries. She handed Pierce a shopping list and a twenty-dollar bill.

He frowned at the money. "I insist," she said firmly, forcibly curving his fingers around the bill.

"Let it be noted that I concede under protest."

"Fine. Just so long as you concede."

She was glad that the kiss that morning hadn't put a wedge of tension between them. By the time they reached the cabin to find the downstairs bed already made and the ones upstairs being worked on, he was conversing as though nothing had happened. She tried to ignore that he went out of his way not to touch her or be alone with her. His avoidance both relieved and piqued her, so it was wiser not to think about it at all.

"Which bed are you going to sleep in, Mommy?" Adam asked, feeling important since it hadn't even been suggested that he stay behind to take a nap rather than accompany David and Pierce. "You can sleep in mine and Pierce's. We wouldn't mind, would we, Pierce?"

The corners of Pierce's lips were twitching with suppressed laughter as he cocked a rakish eyebrow at a blushing Alicia. "No. While we're gone she can sleep in any bed she chooses. She has the run of the place."

"In that case," she said, buttoning up David's jacket and futilely finger-combing his dark hair, "I may make a pallet under the trees."

"You won't either. You'd be afraid of snakes and bugs and stuff."

She tweaked her eldest son on the nose. "You're right."

The boys raced for the jeep, fighting over who would get to sit in the front seat first. "You're sure you don't mind staying alone?"

Her laugh was spontaneous and genuine. "Are you

kidding? Do you know how rare these precious occasions are?"

"Okay," Pierce said. "Just don't open the door to strangers," he warned with a mocking grin.

Alicia waved them off with a glowing feeling warming her from the inside out. But on the fringes of that energy source, away from that tingling heat, there lurked an indefinable sadness.

When she woke from her nap—she had slept in the upstairs twin bed—Pierce and the boys were building a fire in a ring of stones well away from the cabin but not too close to the trees.

"Hey, Mom," David called out when he saw her looking at them from the upstairs window, "we're gonna cook the fish in the coals of the fire. Pierce knows how. Are you coming down now?"

"Have the fish been scaled and gutted?"

"Yes."

"Then I'm coming down."

While they tended the fire and wrapped potatoes, ears of corn, and seasoned fillets of fish in foil, Alicia baked a double batch of tollhouse cookies. "Those smell scrumptious," Pierce said from over her shoulder as she dropped the balls of dough onto the cookie sheet.

"Better than raw fish," she said, wrinkling her nose and sniffing the air.

He laughed. "Just wait till you taste it." Reaching around her, he scooped up a fingerful of the dough from the mixing bowl and plopped it into his mouth. She spun around to confront him.

"Pierce! You're worse than the boys."

"Am I?" His eyes were dancing emeralds of mischief as he laughed down at her. He bent forward quickly and Alicia thought he was going to kiss her, possibly on her nose. But just as suddenly as it had sparked, the light in his eyes went out and he pulled back. Turning away, he went through the screen door and she was left staring after him as she had been that morning, wondering what she had done to turn him off so abruptly.

The boys enjoyed that meal more than any other they had ever eaten. They all ate outside, sitting around the fire. The boys hung onto Pierce's every word as he told them how he had learned to cook over a campfire on a hunting trip with his father. Once again Alicia was grateful to him. She could never have made the week such fun. He was just what her boys needed, a masculine presence, a role model. It was plain to see that they had awarded him a place next to their other heroes, their late father and Carter Madison.

For a man who had never had children, who wasn't even married, Pierce showed infinite patience with them. Unless he was a very good actor, he was enjoying the boys' company as much as they were his. When they talked to him, they held his attention. He gave everything they said importance and credence, when she often tuned out their chatter, listening with half an ear and recording only what she deemed important.

"Off to bed, you two," he said after they had carried the dishes into the cabin.

"Oh, please, can we stay up longer?"

"Nope," Pierce said, shaking his head. "If you go to bed without an argument I may have a surprise for you tomorrow."

"What?"

"Can't tell."

"He can't tell, David, or it wouldn't be a surprise."

Pierce laughed. "That's right, Adam. Good night or no surprise."

After hasty kisses aimed in the general direction of Alicia's mouth, the boys went into the cabin. "More wine?" Pierce asked Alicia once they were alone. Only

the occasional stirring of autumn leaves and the crack-
ling friendliness of the fire broke the pervading quiet.

An aluminum bucket had served as their wine cooler.
He had surprised her with it after dishing up their
campfire supper. "White, of course, madam, to go with
your fish," he had said in a sonorous tone and executed
a stiff formal butler's bow. Alicia's dumbfoundedness
had given way to delight as he poured her a liberal
portion into a tin cup.

"No, thank you," she said now. "It was delicious, but
no more for me."

"Half a glass? It's good for the soul."

"If my soul gets to feeling any better, I'm going to fall
over in a stupor."

He laughed. "A woman who can't hold her liquor,
huh? That could prove dangerous."

They lapsed into silence, smiling, looking at each
other. Then because looking at each other proved to be
unsettling, they stopped looking at each other. Then
stopped smiling. The longer the silence stretched out,
the more awkward it became. Finally Alicia got up,
dusted off the seat of her pants, and said, "In spite of my
nap, I'm sleepy. Thank you for a wonderful dinner,
Pierce. I'll do the dishes before I go upstairs."

How he moved that quickly, she never knew. By the
time she leaned down to pick up her cup of wine and
turned toward the cabin, he was standing inches away
blocking her path.

"I shouldn't have kissed you this morning." His body
was rigid with self-enforced control.

"No," she said, her head down, eyes staring at his
boots, "you shouldn't have."

"I shouldn't kiss you now either."

"No."

"But I'm going to anyway."

Before her reflexes, dulled by the wine, could respond,

she was being folded into his arms and molded against his hard frame. His lips plundered again, but more sweetly this time. They savored her as they whisked back and forth over her mouth before they settled and pressed. His tongue parted her obliging lips to tease the sensitive inner lining. When he heard her murmur of arousal, it plunged deeply and with authority to investigate her mouth at will.

What little resistance she had initially fell away like melting wax. She craved the tutelage of his mouth, for surely she had never been kissed with such expertise. His passion frightened and thrilled her. It reminded her body of its long abstinence from all things sexual. Her sense of shame was diminished by the sweet flow of wine through her veins. She arched against him invitingly.

The sounds he made in his throat were wonderful to her ears. They were guttural, animal, the sounds of a male mating—or desperately wanting to. It was gratifying to her ego that she, a mother, a widow, could excite an exciting man like Pierce.

He left her mouth and swept hot airy kisses on her cheeks and nose, her jaw and earlobes, on her temples and in her hair. One hand slipped past her waist and secured her hips hard against his. The other pushed aside the collar of her shirt. He planted his mouth at the base of her throat. When his lips parted, she felt the scalding caress of his tongue, rasping and velvety at once.

"I swear to you, this is not why I encouraged you to stay," he said thickly. His lips sipped at her neck.

"I know." She didn't remember when she had set down her cup and raised her arms, but now her fingers were tangled in his hair and she was holding his head fast.

"I tried to keep my hands off you. I swear I did. I couldn't any longer."

His mouth met hers in another fiery kiss. An erotically gifted instrument, his tongue made love to her mouth. With rhythmic, wild, savage thrusts he deflowered it and left no question as to his claim of absolute possession. His hand was once more inside her jacket, bolder now than it had been that morning. It tensed around the slimness of her waist and slid up her ribs to mold to the undercurve of her breast. She held her breath.

A long sustained sigh soughed through her lips when his hand covered her with strong warmth. He massaged her through her sweater, rubbing the soft angora wool back and forth over her fevered skin until he felt her nipple bud in his palm. He pressed it with his thumb, circled it, stroked.

"Oh, God." He strained the curse through clenched teeth and Alicia bit back a protest of outrage and frustration when he released her and stepped away. He turned his back. She ran for the cabin and let the door slam behind her. Fury and humiliation battled within her. Never in her life had she felt both emotions so keenly.

It took long minutes before she was restored. She forced herself across the room to the kitchen area where she methodically began to wash dishes. She wasn't about to run upstairs and hide her shame like a thwarted teenager. Rejection tasted brassy and bitter in her mouth, but she'd be damned before she'd let him know it.

He stepped through the door. "Are you all right?"

Her whole body was flashing hotly and freezing cold, her nerves were in pandemonium, she was quaking with unrequited desire, all five senses were shooting off like skyrockets and he wanted to know if she was all right. At that moment she hated him and could barely garner enough civility to gnash out, "Of course. As you said, you shouldn't have kissed me. It was better to end it there. No hard feelings."

Frustrated in his own right, his arm shot out and he wound a handful of her hair around his fist and pulled her around to face him. Amazingly it was almost a caress of tenderness, for he didn't hurt her.

He didn't speak until she raised hostile eyes to meet his. "I wanted to kiss you, Alicia, and to go on kissing you." He pulled her closer, still not making his hold painful. "And I didn't want it to end there. I didn't want it to end until we had made love so many times we were exhausted. Can't you tell how much I want you?"

She could now, now that he had moved closer still and the lower part of his body was stamped against her thigh. He laid his hard cheek along hers; his lips moved against her temple. Every pore of his body secreted anguish, a pain she couldn't identify. "It's important to me that you know how much I want you and that my reasons for not making love to you are insurmountable. Otherwise . . ." He heaved a regretful sigh and stepped back. Gradually he let go of her hair. He studied her face, all but flaying off the skin and reading her every thought with those piercing green eyes. Then he said abjectly, "Go upstairs. I'll finish up here."

She didn't dare argue. If she stayed with him for as long as another heartbeat, she might very well make a fool of herself and beg him to take her despite whatever problems prevented it.

What could it be?

Alicia studied Pierce from the upstairs window. It was early. Miraculously she had awakened before the boys and hadn't been able to go back to sleep as she reviewed the disturbing events of the night before.

Pierce had been jogging this morning. His warm-up

suit was drenched with sweat. Obviously he had driven himself to the limit of his endurance. He was propped against a tree, staring up through its branches. His face was twisted with his private turmoil. He wiped perspiration out of his eyes and Alicia heard him curse.

Whatever it was that tormented him, whatever that insurmountable obstacle was, it was terrible and something he couldn't eliminate with his own resources.

Alicia couldn't let it worry her. At the end of the week they would go their separate ways. In the meantime, she had her own problem to grapple with and solve. Her mind must remain occupied solely with that.

Yet, looking down at Pierce's bowed head, she confessed that objectivity where he was concerned had vanished the moment he had kissed her. Whether or not he had invited her to be, whether or not he wanted her to be, she was already involved.

The surprise he had promised the boys turned out to be mopeds, which Alicia was coerced into riding. They rode doubles, David behind Pierce and Adam clinging to her waist and demanding that she go faster.

The next day it rained in the morning and Pierce entertained the boys with games of checkers and lessons on whittling until the sun came out. Alicia baked brownies and made a savory stew for their supper. They checked on the other cabin and saw that the repairs had been done satisfactorily. No one suggested that Alicia and the boys should move to it, but during those two days, Pierce didn't make a romantic overture. Their relationship returned to that of friendly companionship. What took place after their cookout might well never have happened.

"I'd like to stay close to the cabin today, if you think we can keep the boys busy." They were having a last cup of morning coffee. David and Adam had finished the chores Pierce had assigned them and were playing with a soccer ball in front of the cabin.

"Sure. Whatever. Please don't feel you have to entertain us every minute. If there's something you want to do by yourself—"

"It's not that." He set his cup aside and she could tell he was uneasy. "I'm expecting a guest tonight for dinner."

"Oh, Pierce, you should have said something sooner!" She leaped out of her chair like a wound-up spring let go. "We'll leave immediately and make the cabin available—"

"Sit down," he said, laughing and grabbing her wrist and forcing her back into the chair she had vacated. "I want you to stay and be here for dinner."

She looked at him dubiously. "When you have company coming?"

His eyes locked into hers. "It's not actually company. It's my daughter."

# *Four*

Chrissy Reynolds arrived as the sun was sinking behind the woods. Braking a red Porsche to a stop in front of the cabin, the tall, attractive, slender young woman alighted. She was welcomed by David and Adam who, disregarding Alicia's instructions that they not race out the door, bounded through it and down the steps to admire the car that was to them the ultimate status symbol.

"Well, hello." Chrissy laughed as she was flanked by the boys, each of whom were staring up at her curiously. "Do I have the right cabin?"

"Yes, you do." Pierce took the front steps down to greet his daughter. Though he walked with a somewhat calmer stride, he was just as anxious to see her as the boys had been. "Hello, Chrissy."

Watching from behind the security of the screen, Alicia saw Chrissy's smile brighten bashfully. "Hello, Daddy," Alicia heard her say hesitantly. His daughter was actually shy of him. Alicia didn't wonder at this after what Pierce had told her that morning.

"Your daughter!" she had exclaimed almost sound-lessly. "Your *daughter*?" She had sprung out of the chair again and for the second time he pulled her back down. She yanked her hand away but remained seated. "You told me you didn't have any children."

The first thing she suspected was that he had a wife and God knew how many children waiting for him at home. She might have had one fling in Tahoe since her husband's death, but that was the extent of her romantic adventures. Being kissed and kissing back a married man was something else again.

She was hurt beyond reason and out of proportion to the extent that she was involved with Pierce. He hadn't seemed the type to lie so deviously.

"Alicia, don't jump to conclusions before you hear me out. I told you I'd had no part of parenting. I never said I didn't have a child. My wife and I divorced soon after Chrissy's birth. I abdicated my responsibility of rearing her to her mother, something that I bitterly regret. I wanted to see my daughter this week. It's become very important that I spend time with her. That's why I invited her to come up here one evening and have dinner with me."

She had been mollified, but still felt that he had misled her. "We'll leave before she arrives. I'm sure she won't expect you to have other guests when you made a special point of inviting her to join you."

"She doesn't expect anything one way or another. I wasn't exaggerating how I neglected her while she was growing up. The occasions she's visited me are embarrassingly few in number. Her mother and I can barely tolerate the sight of each other, so at the time the custody papers were being drawn up, it seemed best for all concerned if I stayed out of their lives."

Instinctive female curiosity began to crawl over Alicia like an annoying tiny insect that one can't see, but can feel. She tried to brush it away. But she'd been bit. She was dying to know the details of his marriage and its breakup. However, if a man didn't even call his ex-wife by her first name, he wasn't going to talk about her. Alicia had remained silent.

"I thought I'd cook beef stroganoff for dinner," he said. "Do you think that will be okay?"

He was nervous! She could tell by the anxiety lacing that otherwise innocuous question that Pierce had misgivings about this reunion with his daughter. That vulnerability, so unusual in a man with Pierce's confidence, touched a chord deep inside her.

"Beef stroganoff sounds delicious," she assured him softly. "Pierce, are you sure you want us around tonight?"

"Yes," he answered swiftly. Too swiftly.

"To act as buffers? Are you expecting a fight? A scene?"

His grin was lopsided and self-deprecating. "No. Nothing like that. I just want it to be a pleasant evening for her, that's all."

"I'll fix something special for dessert."

"No, no. Don't feel that you have to do that."

"I don't. I've got a sweet tooth."

He knew better, but he accepted her generous offer with appreciation.

Now as Alicia watched father and daughter embrace, she could tell such displays of affection were infrequent and awkward for them both. Pierce hugged Chrissy to him, but briefly. He pushed her away to look at her. "You look terrific as always. Did you get your hair cut? I like it."

"Do you? Thanks. Mother had a fit. She didn't want it cut before the wedding."

*Wedding?* Whose wedding? Hers or her mother's?

"The big day is fast approaching. Any premarital jitters?"

Ah-h, Chrissy was the bride-to-be.

"A few," she admitted with a soft laugh. "But that's natural, I guess."

Pierce's brows knitted as he studied his daughter. He sensed that she could elaborate but had chosen to be reticent. He swung an arm around her shoulders. "I don't know if I'm willing to give you away yet or not."

The girl's face glowed with happy surprise, and Alicia saw tears standing in her eyes—eyes like her father's. "Thank you for inviting me up here this week, Daddy. I needed an evening away from . . . everything."

He squeezed her shoulder. "We should have done more of this long ago. I'm just now realizing how much of you I've missed. Old age has the advantage of wisdom, I guess."

She poked him in the ribs. "You're hardly sliding over the far side of the hill." She glanced down at David and Adam. "And you've sure got young friends."

"Pardon my rudeness," Pierce said, laughing. "Chrissy, my friends David and Adam Russell. Boys, my daughter."

"She sure is old," Adam said. They were disappointed. When they had been told Pierce's daughter was coming for dinner, they had obviously conjured up an image of someone closer to their age, not an ancient twenty-one-year-old.

Chrissy put her hands on her hips. "She's not too old to play soccer. Whose ball is that?" She pointed to the ball that had rolled beneath an evergreen bush.

"Mine," David said, his frown lifting slightly. "I'll let you play with it if you'll let me ride in your Porsche. It's super. I have a poster of one in my room. I wanted Mom to buy one but she said it wasn't prac . . . part . . . pract—"

"Practical," Pierce supplied and Chrissy laughed.

"Well, she's smarter than Daddy then. He gave it to me last Christmas. You've got a deal about the soccer ball and the car." Chrissy turned to her father and gave him an arch look. "Have you known David and Adam long?"

"Since Sunday night. I rescued them during a thunderstorm."

"You're kidding!"

"No, he's not. He did!" David said.

"Yeah, he carried us and Mom back to his house and it was raining real hard and lightning, but I wasn't scared," Adam added.

Chrissy had also inherited her father's expressive eyebrows. One curved high as she eyed him shrewdly. "Well, the boys are certainly cute. How about Mom?"

Alicia blushed to the roots of her hair and tried to duck into the shadows of the cabin before she could be caught eavesdropping. But Pierce turned around and called out to her. She had no choice but to push through the screen door and take the steps down to be formally introduced.

"Alicia Russell, my daughter Chrissy."

"Hello, Chrissy," Alicia said, suddenly feeling like a scarlet woman. And why? She, better than anyone, knew that nothing had happened between her and this girl's father. But how would Chrissy react to her and the boys sharing Pierce's cabin?

"Hi. It's nice to meet you." Her smile was wide, pleasant, friendly, and guileless. "Did he really rescue you during a thunderstorm?"

"I hate to admit it, but yes. And when we couldn't find other lodging after our borrowed cabin was damaged by the storm, he insisted we share his." Alicia felt compelled to explain quickly, lest Chrissy draw the wrong conclusion.

Mischievously Chrissy slid her eyes in her father's

direction. "He's a regular knight in shining armor," she commented dryly, but without rancor.

No matter about Alicia's rapid explanation, Chrissy had summed up the situation in her own mind the moment she saw Alicia. She might not know much about her father, but she knew that he was a connoisseur of women. Alicia Russell's wholesomeness was a departure from the kind of woman he usually squired around. Nonetheless the sexual currents radiating between them were real and alive and popping. Stand too close when they looked at each other, and you could get singed.

"What's a night in shiny armor?" Adam asked.

"Why don't we discuss that over a cold drink?" Pierce suggested, and began shepherding everyone inside.

Alicia liked Chrissy immediately. She was chatty and animated, shy only when she looked directly at her father. It was as though she wanted to fling her arms around him and hold him tight but was afraid to. It was apparent every time she looked at him that she admired him and loved him, but that she didn't feel completely comfortable around him either. Alicia got the impression that the young woman desperately wanted his approval and affection.

Chrissy enlightened them on her progress in art school, and because she aspired to design women's clothing, she and Alicia launched into a long discussion on fashion.

Bored, David whined, "Can we play soccer now?"

Pierce stood. "You ladies excuse us. I'll take them out and run off some of their energy."

"No," Chrissy said, rising. "I promised. Come on boys." They raced out ahead of her.

"Your daughter is lovely, Pierce. A vibrant, intelligent young woman."

"Isn't she?" he said proudly as he watched her

through the screen door. "I only wish I could claim some credit for the way she's turned out."

"You can."

He shook his head. "I was never around. She deserved a father, a good one, one she knew cared about her. What happened between her mother and me wasn't her fault, but she's the one who paid for it."

"I think she knew you were there if she needed you," Alicia said quietly.

He turned to her and his green eyes speared straight through her. "I'd like to believe that, Alicia. I need to believe that."

"She doesn't seem to be holding a grudge. She looks at you with love, not resentment. Maybe she needs to hear how you feel about her. Have you ever told her you love her?" He pondered that for a moment, his brows drawn together. "Go on out with them and I'll set the table for dinner."

"I can't leave you to do all the work."

She pointed toward the door. "Go." She used the same no-nonsense and no-backtalk voice she used on her boys.

"Yes, ma'am." Before she could react he smacked a sound kiss on her mouth and went out the screen door.

Twenty minutes later Alicia called the boys inside for a bath before dinner. They complained and grumbled, but she finally got them indoors and into the bathroom. She carried a tray with two glasses and a bottle of chilled white wine out to Pierce and Chrissy who had collapsed in fatigue on the front steps.

"I'm sorry this is all we have in the way of a predinner drink," Alicia said, setting the tray down.

"Where's your glass?" Pierce asked, patting the spot beside him on the porch to indicate that she should sit down.

"I'm supervising the bathing or they might flood the

bathroom. Take your time. The rolls still have to bake. I'll call you when dinner is ready."

Pierce reached up and touched her hand. "Thank you." His look carried with it gratitude and something else. He was grateful to her for providing him and his daughter this moment alone. And the something else? Alicia couldn't quite define it, but it made her insides seem anchorless.

As she was putting the food on the table, they came in hand in hand. Chrissy was saying, "That was the Christmas you sent me the pony, remember? I've never seen Mother so furious. I only got to keep it for one day before she sent it back to the stables."

"She's always been a b-i-t-c-h."

"I know what that spells," David piped. "Bitch."

"David Russell!" Alicia was horrified.

Pierce looked embarrassed and Chrissy said, "See what calling Mother bad names can get you?"

"It wasn't a bad name. It was a factual name. And I'm not sorry I said it, only sorry that David heard it. It's an impolite word, David, so don't let me hear you using it."

"Yes, sir."

Dinner was a happy time. The group lacked for nothing to talk about. Pierce had done an excellent job on the stroganoff, though he complimented Alicia on boiling the noodles to just the right tenderness. She missed the frequent entertaining she and Jim had done and had put all her culinary talents into a lemon meringue pie that won everyone's approval.

The boys hadn't forgotten the promised ride in the Porsche. Chrissy handed Pierce the keys. "Will you do the honors while I help Alicia with the dishes?"

"That isn't necessary," Alicia said quickly.

"I want to. We didn't get to finish our debate about next year's hem lengths."

"Then I'm all too glad to take the boys out." Pierce

hooked a young Russell under each arm and carried them screeching gleefully out the front door.

Chrissy caught Alicia fondly and wistfully smiling after them. Embarrassed, she began clearing the table. "I understand you're getting married soon. What kind of gown have you picked out?"

Chrissy described her gown and the color scheme she had chosen for the wedding. Conversation was no effort between them. Alicia found herself telling the younger woman about Jim and his death, her life as a widow, her job, even about Sloan and Carter.

"Have you slept with Daddy?"

That was something else Chrissy had inherited from her father, the ability to shock one speechless with an incisive, out-of-context question.

Alicia's hands were submerged in the soapy water. At the audacious, presumptuous question, they balled into fists. "No," she said softly. Lifting her eyes to Chrissy, she repeated slowly, "No, I haven't."

"I think you should," Chrissy remarked. She wasn't looking at Alicia, but was concentrating on lining up the glassware in the cabinet.

Alicia couldn't believe the girl's candor. "Why?"

Chrissy looked at her, smiled, and shrugged. "Why not? You obviously find each other attractive. Don't get me wrong. I don't believe in sleeping around. I just think . . ." She paused to stare into space for a moment. Then she turned to Alicia again. And just as Alicia quelled under Pierce's steady stare, so did she under Chrissy's, for they were identical. One couldn't hide one's thoughts from those eyes. "There's something wrong with Daddy."

"Wrong? What do you mean?"

"I don't know. He's different. Even his inviting me up here is uncharacteristic. Always before on my visits, he's been in a hurry. I got tired just trying to keep up with

him. He was always moving. Now he's meditative, senti-
mental. He's doing things that aren't like him at all."

"Like inviting a poor widow and her sons to stay the
week with him?"

Chrissy laughed and boldly assessed Alicia's shape.
"Surely you've figured out why he did that. If you had
looked like a troll, I'm sure he would have been polite
and seen that you were safe, but I doubt if he would have
been quite so hospitable." Discomfited, Alicia looked
away. Chrissy took her hand and forced Alicia's eyes
back to hers. "If he asks you, will you sleep with him?"

Alicia swallowed, too overcome by surprise to be
offended. "I don't know."

"I hope you will. I think he needs you."

"I'm sure a man like your father doesn't lack for female
company."

"I'm sure he doesn't either. I'm not talking about sex.
Not exclusively anyway. I think he needs all that you are,
your warmth, compassion. And I think being with him
would do you a world of good too."

Alicia thankfully heard the return of the Porsche and
was glad the conversation couldn't go any further. The
boys were put to bed upstairs so the adults could con-
tinue their visit. They bid a solemn farewell to Chrissy,
and Alicia knew they hoped to see her again. She knelt
down and kissed their cheeks and neither moved away
from the caress they usually avoided whenever possible.

It was late when Chrissy said she had to start back.

"Do you have to?" Pierce questioned. "We could make
room for you."

"I have a class in the morning and a wedding gown fit-
ting at noon. Mother would freak if I didn't show up for
that." She took both Alicia's hands. "It was so nice to
meet you. I'm officially inviting you and the boys to the
wedding."

"Thank you. We'll see."

Chrissy shocked Alicia then by pulling her into a swift hug.

"Remember what I said. I give you my permission." Chrissy winked before she turned away and Alicia avoided Pierce's inquiring eyes.

"I'll walk her to her car," he said.

For half an hour, Alicia sat in front of the fireplace, flipping through a magazine. Their voices occasionally drifted in to her. Once she thought she heard Chrissy crying, but couldn't be sure. At last she heard the growl of the Porsche's engine and the crunch of tires as it rolled onto the narrow gravel road.

Pierce was a long time coming in and, sensing that he might wish to be alone, Alicia headed for the stairs. She certainly didn't want him to think she had waited up for him. Her foot had just touched the bottom step when he came in.

"Are you going to bed?"

"Yes, I thought—"

He stretched out his hand. "Will you sit with me for a while, Alicia?"

Her heart began to beat heavily and she couldn't say exactly why. Perhaps because it was quiet and they were alone. Perhaps it was because she had turned out all the lights save one soft lamp and the cabin was dim and whispered intimacy from every corner. Perhaps it was because of his slightly raspy, highly emotional voice and the way he had spoken her name. For whatever reason, she was trembling with feeling as she retraced her steps to the sofa and took the hand held out for her. He pulled her down beside him on the deep, age-soft cushions.

"Thank you for taking over the dinner."

"It was nothing. No, really," she said when she noted his skeptical look. "I enjoyed playing hostess."

"Well, anyway, I appreciate it. I think Chrissy had a

good time. It temporarily took her mind off the circus her mother is making out of her wedding."

Alicia squelched common sense and ventured onto ground she knew was as potentially explosive as a minefield. She trod softly. "Chrissy doesn't seem very excited about her wedding. Does she love her fiancé?"

"I think she must feel some affection for him. He's not a disagreeable young man. But I don't think she loves him."

"Then why—"

"She's being pushed into a 'good marriage.' Good by her mother's standards, that is."

"I see."

"No, you don't, but I'd like to explain. It's a long, boring story."

"I'm not doing anything else," she said, smiling, sensing his need to talk.

"You could be sleeping."

"I'd rather listen."

"I can't unload on you."

"I talked out my problem with you the other night. Sometimes strangers are the best listeners."

"Are we still strangers?" She was the first to look away from a long, puissant stare. He sighed heavily. "Okay, here goes. I married young and foolishly. Dottie considered me a good catch, a promising engineer. She had a pretty face, a terrific body, and an obliging attitude toward sex. I walked into a velvet trap and she sank her claws into me before I knew I'd been had. We were mismatched. We had different goals, different priorities. It was doomed to failure."

He went on to explain that his wife, who had come from an affluent family, got extremely upset when he put most of his savings and a small legacy into a new, struggling engineering firm rather than going with an already established one. Money was tight and they could no longer be members of the country club and move with that set. Then she had gotten pregnant.

"I was made to feel like a sexual deviate whose lust wouldn't let him take time for contraceptives, when in fact our bed was the only place we were the least bit compatible." Alicia swallowed a knot and was alarmed to discover that it was cold, rank jealousy. "I threatened to kill her if she even thought about an abortion. By today's standards I'm sure my attitude would seem intolerant and incredibly puritanical. Nonetheless, that's how I felt. How I still feel.

"Soon after Chrissy was born, we agreed that our lives would be much happier if we never saw each other again. Dottie hates me for causing the one failure in her life. I'm the only thing she ever wanted, went after, but couldn't have."

He ran his hands through his hair. "But I blame myself for the failed marriage because I never should have married her in the first place. And as a parent, well, that speaks for itself. I don't even know my daughter. I missed her childhood, her youth, her adolescence. Now she's gotten herself committed to a marriage that is going to make her miserably unhappy and I can't do a damned thing to stop it. Any interference on my part would be like declaring World War III with Dottie. Yet I feel that I have to do this one important thing for my daughter before—" He broke off suddenly.

"Before what?"

"Never mind. It's just that I think she wants help in getting out of this mess and doesn't know how to ask for it. I told her to stand up to her mother. I know she won't."

"Chrissy's an intelligent woman. She won't be forced into a marriage she doesn't want."

"You don't know Dottie. She's as shrewd a strategist as George Patton. And about as humanitarian as Nero.

When she sets her mind to something, people have a way of cowering and going along to prevent a fight."

"You didn't."

His head swiveled around and his eyes held her motionless. "No, thank God I didn't. I only hope Chrissy will see her mistake in time. Hell, her mother wants that young man for a son-in-law because of his last name. She probably harbors a terrible dislike for him and can't wait to rearrange his life too. Everyone but Dottie will be unhappy."

"When the time comes, Chrissy will know what to do."

"Will she? She won't have me to thank if she does. I've salved my conscience for being a lousy parent by giving her presents—ponies and Porsches. I've never given her guidance, a sense of values, anything that's really important. God, it's a wonder she doesn't despise me."

Of its own volition, Alicia's hand stroked back strands of disheveled hair that lay silvery-brown on his forehead. They slid through her fingers in a silky caress. "You're not the reprobate you paint yourself to be, Pierce. And don't worry about Chrissy. She's got a good head on her shoulders."

"I told her tonight that I loved her," he said in a low voice.

So, her subtly given advice had been taken. "What did she do?"

He smiled. "She cried and hugged me and told me that she loved me too."

"I'm glad, Pierce. Very glad for both of you."

He raised one knee so he could face her. Leaning forward, he searched her eyes. "I have you to thank for tonight's success. I can't tell you how important it was to me."

"It would have happened sooner or later. You wanted it to. So did Chrissy. I only gave you a nudge to do something you already planned to do."

He touched her cheek with his fingertips. "What makes you so easy to talk to? So understanding? So tuned in to other people and what makes them tick?"

"I'm not. I've never been anything but purely selfish."

"I find that hard to believe." His voice was deep and soft and low. It touched her in places that shouldn't be touched, like her breasts, her stomach, and between her thighs. She felt his voice in each erogenous spot like a kittenish, lapping caress.

"Believe it. I've been known to think only of myself, otherwise I wouldn't have always turned my life over to other people to take care of. First my parents, then Jim. I didn't worry about anything but my own happiness and what they would do to bring it about. When I lost Jim I transferred the responsibility for my life to Carter. It's safer to do that, you see. Then you can't be blamed when things go wrong."

She shook her head sadly and for emphasis she covered his hand with her own. "Pierce, deep inside I knew Carter didn't love me, even before he met Sloan. I almost let him ruin his life, destroy his chance at happiness, in order to secure my own future."

"Don't be so hard on yourself. You had your boys to think of."

"I used them as my excuse." Lost in her own thoughts, she fiddled with the buttons on his shirt. The familiarity didn't seem at all unnatural. "I finally woke up to the fact that I was an adult, that I had to take full responsibility for my life and that of my sons. For the first time in my life I'm standing on my own two feet. I like myself better for it, but it's a shaky perch at times."

"I don't know anyone who doesn't feel afraid at one time or another." His eyes turned introspective, and for a moment she thought that he might draw away again. Instead he raised her hand to his mouth and pressed his lips against her palm. "What did you and Chrissy talk about?"

He must have felt her pulse leap beneath his stroking thumb on her wrist because his eyes lifted to hers. His lashes were dark and long and ridiculously lavish. She wanted to run her finger over them. "Girl talk. Nothing much."

"Did she ask about us?"

"Yes."

"What did she want to know?"

She knew where the truthful answer might lead. In this instance, it would be best to avoid the truth. But she didn't want to. She wanted to be led straight into the jaws of temptation. Damn the consequences. "Chrissy asked me if we were sleeping together."

"What did you tell her?"

"I told her no."

"What did she say to that?"

Alicia wet her lips with the tip of her tongue. Jealously he watched it disappear back between her lips. "She said she thought we should, that it would be good for both of us."

"I'm inclined to agree. I know it would be damned good for me." He cupped her face between his hands and drilled into her eyes with the hot, emerald brilliance of his. He saw in her eyes a need, a longing, a desire as clamorous as his own. "What about you?"

"I think it would be mutually satisfying." The die was cast.

"I can't get involved. It would be bed, that's all. I don't want you to be hurt later."

"I understand."

"Do you? Do you, Alicia? Because I have to know now."

"I can't get involved with anyone either."

"We're two people who know what we're doing, right? Consenting adults."

"Yes."

"No regrets later."

"No regrets."

"It's only for tonight. Nothing binding. We attach no special significance to it, just take it for what it is, a physical release, a pleasurable exchange of flesh. Right?"

"Yes." The last word came out a plea as passionate as the way her body curved longingly against his.

His thumbs outlined her lips, detailed their shape before his mouth took them under his kiss. Without preamble or apology, his tongue pressed into her mouth and moved freely, rampantly, stroking, delving, tasting all of her.

Wrapping his arms around her, he stood and brought her to her feet. Never letting his mouth leave hers, he held her full length against him and carried her to the bed. He let her slide to her feet and the dragging motion of her body along his brought moans of desire from their throats. Deftly he tugged her shirttail free of her waistband.

He ducked his head and kissed her breasts through the cloth even as he unbuttoned her blouse. When he parted the garment and peeled it down her shoulders her breasts were damp from his mouth and their crests were rosy and taut beneath her sheer brassiere.

Forcibly he calmed himself, commanded himself to slow down, not to ravage but to savor. His hands closed with tender possessiveness around her breasts and he fondled her with gently squeezing motions.

"You are wonderful to touch," he whispered along her neck.

Her hands folded around his neck and she laid her cheek against his thudding heart. He smelled of that elusive, expensive, woodsy cologne and she breathed it in greedily.

Nimbly his hands went around her back and unfastened her brassiere. When he pulled it away from her and dropped it to the floor, she faced him demurely. But his eyes showered praise on her. "Your breasts are beautiful, Alicia. Beautiful."

His eyes, his words, then his hands and lips testified to that. He brushed light kisses on the soft flesh, lifting her breasts to his mouth with his palms. Her nipples beaded beneath the sweet coaxing of his fingertips and his tongue circled them in lazy contrast to the fury building inside them both.

"Do you want to undress yourself?" he asked, his throat throbbing with self-imposed restraint.

"Do you want to undress me?"

"Very much."

She stepped out of her shoes and stood before him, compliant. His eyes rained liquid heat on her as they slid over her tremulous breasts, down her stomach to her waist. He released the slender belt and slowly unbuttoned and unzipped the flannel slacks she had worn for Chrissy's visit. Putting his hands inside them on either side of her hips, he lowered them down her legs until she could step out of them.

"I already knew your legs were beautiful," he whispered playfully as he straightened. Hooking his thumbs in the elastic of her panties, he started to pull them down. He felt her tense suddenly and immediately withdrew his hands. "Did I do something wrong?"

"No, it's just . . ." Embarrassed by her sudden attack of virginal modesty she sought to make amends by laying her hands on his chest and unbuttoning his shirt. His chest hair looked fuzzy in the soft light and she longed to rub her face in it but didn't quite have the courage. He stood still and let her examine him. His nipples were dark and flat. Inquisitively she touched one with the tip of her finger and it distended. His breath hissed through his teeth. Was that good or bad? She never remembered touching Jim there.

*I'm no good at this,* she thought dismally. *He won't like me. I don't know the right things to do.* She and Jim had been married before the sexual liberation of women. Now she felt ignorant and callow and distressed.

Sensing it, Pierce lay comforting hands on her shoulders. "Why don't you lie down."

She turned toward the bed and folded back the covers while he took off the rest of his clothes. She lay down, refusing to look at him, though she could see from the corner of her eye that he was naked. He approached the bed and knelt on it with one knee.

"Alicia?" he asked softly. He bent down and took one of her hands and laid it high on his thigh. She squeezed her eyes shut and her chest heaved with fear. He rubbed the back of her hand with his palm. "Do you want to stop? Tell me."

The concern in his tone compelled her to look at him. She saw his sleek nakedness, the intriguing dusting of body hair, the corded muscles, the toasty skin, the masculine strength.

But stronger than his desire, than his body, was his character. Even now, he was willing to let her call it off. An emotion feeling very much like love welled in her throat. She remembered his talking with her boys, making them sit still with rapt attention, making them squeal with laughter. She remembered the times she had caught him looking at her with tenderness, a yearning that surpassed sexual desire. Despite what he had said about himself, he was kind and caring and she wanted to experience this man.

Slowly her fingers curved around the outside of his

thigh and she moved her hand in a light caress. "No, I don't want to stop."

Without haste, he lay down beside her and gathered her beneath him. He held her for a long time before he kissed her. When he did, his lips honored hers softly and she relaxed against him. Sliding his hands down her torso, he removed her panties, taking care to go slow, not to frighten her.

His eyes took in her nakedness and she lay submissive beneath them. When he looked again into her eyes, his were shining with pleasure and his smile was a silent endearment. He caressed her earnestly, unhurriedly, delaying the supreme gratification by heightening the anticipation. Her body hummed and purred beneath his hands and lips.

He watched his hands as they smoothed over her skin, visually enhancing his pleasure in her. Alicia marveled that she wasn't burning with embarrassment. Rather, her own arousal was embellished by watching his every move, meeting his eyes with a lover's gaze.

With a soft touch he parted her thighs and acquainted himself with her mystery. Alicia felt like a rare treasure being discovered by someone who could appreciate her rarity. She was malleable and moist to his seeking fingertips and he murmured his approval as he moved above her. Alicia felt his passion, hard, so hard. It rubbed against the nest of tawny hair between her thighs. His lips were softly urgent against her breasts, on her nipples.

He made no lunging, thrusting motions, but suddenly she felt his intrusion and arched against that sublime, invading pressure. He filled her competently, completely, and the pleasure of his possession went on and on, rippling over her like trickles of sensation from a magic waterfall.

"Oh God, it's good," he whispered in her ear. "So good, Alicia."

"Pierce." Softly she cried his name as he began to stroke her with shallow thrusts that gradually deepened. Frantically, her hands groped along his shoulders. Her body bowed and bucked. Had she just forgotten or had it ever felt like this before?

"Shhh," he said quietly without breaking that tantalizing rhythm. "We're in no hurry. This isn't a contest. Relax. Just let it happen, darling. Feel me love you. Just feel."

That's all she could do. Her insides coiled tighter and tighter as he reached higher and higher inside her to touch the very gate of her womanhood. She didn't want to make a fool of herself or do anything she'd be ashamed of later, but when she felt herself quicken and knew that she was about to be swept away on a tidal wave of emotion, her limbs curled around him and she burrowed her face in his chest. "Pierce!" she called as her world exploded into dazzling fragments.

From far away she heard his own soft cries and they were all her name. And they were exultant and . . . sad.

# *Five*

He twined golden strands of hair around his fingers and tried to count the jeweled facets in her eyes. He kissed the plump curve of her breast, nuzzled it. "You're so sweet." The words vaporized damply on her skin.

"Am I?"

"Very, very, very." He punctuated the confirmation with tiny kisses on her throat. Shifting his weight, he resettled them against the pillows. "How long since Jim died?"

"Three years."

"You've been three years without a lover?"

"What makes you say that?" Had she been that unpracticed and awkward? Her body strained away from his.

He smiled affectionately and drew her back close beside him. "I could tell, but it's certainly nothing to be defensive about." His lips wandered along her hairline and his hand seesawed in the deep valley of her waist between ribs and hip. "It's a nice thing to know."

His saying that pleased her and she snuggled closer. "There was one," she confessed quietly.

"Carter."

She lay her hand on his chest and let her fingers idly strum through the crinkly forest of hair. Smiling privately, she hoped that the trace of jealousy in his voice wasn't a product of her imagination. "No, not Carter."

"Not Carter?"

She shook her head. "I told you my relationship with Carter wasn't like that. If we had ever made love, even if we had been married, I think we would have felt like we were betraying Jim. Carter and I were too good friends to be lovers."

"Then there was someone else?"

"He wasn't a 'someone.' He was one night, that's all. He was very nice, but it meant nothing beyond waking me up to the fact that I wasn't dead even though Jim was. And that I was being unfair to myself by taking the first man available to me. Not to mention how unfair it was to Carter."

For long moments Pierce lay quietly. His hands were no longer adoringly caressing her. He barely breathed. Had she been wrong to tell him about that night in Tahoe?

"You lied to me, Alicia."

Startled, she propped herself up and peered down into his shadowed face. "Lied?"

He wrapped his hand around the back of her neck and massaged it lovingly. Her hair was a magnet that attracted every ray of light as it tumbled around his hand and arm, down onto his chest. "You lied when you said tonight wouldn't have any special significance." Knotting handfuls of hair in his fingers, he pulled her face down for his kiss. It was an infinitely tender one. "For you this is more than just sex, isn't it? It means something?"

He watched her eyelids lower, watched the diamond-like tears form on the thick row of lashes, watched as she once again lifted those swimming eyes to his. "Yes. It does," she said hoarsely. "It would have to or I wouldn't be here."

"Alicia." He encircled her waist with his arm and pulled her atop him. The soft weight of her breasts was cushioned against his chest. The slender columns of her thighs aligned to his. This time the kiss wasn't so tender. Every measure of passion he gave, she returned.

Her lips were throbbing and moist when at last they were released. Pierce's, too, were damp. She ran her finger along his lower lip, taking up the moisture, loving the feel of his mouth, loving the taste of herself that lingered on it. "Were you lying, too, Pierce?"

He pressed her head into the hollow of his shoulder. His eyes closed against the exquisite pleasure of holding her nakedness against his. His hands smoothed down the satiny length of her back and over the firm roundness of her derrière. He stroked the backs of her thighs and when he heard that rattling sigh in her throat, he knew that he would make love to her again. Again. And again.

"Yes. To you and to myself, I was lying."


Just before dawn Alicia left Pierce sleeping, gathered her scattered clothes, made a brief stop in the bathroom, and crept upstairs. She slipped on her nightgown and managed to get into bed with Adam without waking him. She felt ridiculous, sneaking into bed like a teenager who had come home too late, but morality was hard enough to teach children these days. If she were ambiguous about last night, how would her boys have taken her sleeping with Pierce?

It seemed that she had only just fallen asleep when she

heard them begin to stir. Whispering, they went down-stairs. Moments later she heard the commode flush. Then she heard Pierce's low, "Hey, are you two already up? Is your mother still sleeping?"

She would have to get up and face them all sooner or later, but she stayed beneath the light covers dreading that time. What was Pierce thinking of her now? What did she think of herself? Why one minute was she breathless and giddy over what had happened between them last night, and the next minute scaldingly ashamed of it?

Nothing in her adult life had prepared her for sharing a bed with Pierce. There wasn't an inch of her body that he hadn't explored thoroughly and didn't now know intimately. Jim had been a sweet, earnest lover, but their bed had been modest and immature compared to the sheer ecstasy of Pierce's.

His lovemaking utilized his whole body, not just his hands and lips and sex, but his skin and hair and all five senses, his heart, and his mind. Perhaps it had been his total concentration on her that made her feel that no woman in history had ever been so loved.

Recollections of all that she'd done, all that had been done to her, made her blush like a maiden aunt. People who knew her well would be shocked by her wanton behavior and boundless responses. Her parents, her friends, Sloan and Carter. Well, maybe not Sloan and Carter, she thought with a smile, remembering the sex-ual passages in Carter's recent books.

But that was them and this was her. A new her. One she had only met. The old Alicia Russell was delighted, and horrified, and intrigued by the woman in her who had emerged last night.

She had put it off long enough. Breakfast was already in full swing downstairs. It was time she joined them.

She pulled on a velour sweat suit, ran a brush through her hair, and timorously approached the steep stairwell.

Adam spotted her first. "Hi, Mom. Did I kick you last night?" He turned to Pierce. "Every time I sleep with her she says I kick."

"I didn't notice it last night." She didn't quite look at Pierce who was leaning against the drainboard sipping coffee. Her nervous eyes merely glanced over him. He had pulled on a pair of jeans, but his chest and feet were bare. Her heart picked up its tempo and her stomach did a cartwheel. She knew the texture of his skin, knew how his body hair felt against her palms and cheeks and lips.

"Good morning, David."

"Hi. Your face is red."

"It is?" Alicia clapped her hands up to her burning cheeks. Her hands were icy.

"Why is your face red, Mom?" Adam asked around a slurpy spoonful of cereal.

"I—I don't know."

"You're sure acting funny," David commented. "Pass the jam please."

Alicia lunged for the jar of grape jam, wishing she could clout her son on the head with it. It took a long, awkward moment before she had enough gumption to look at Pierce.

"Coffee?" he said softly.

And that was enough. His eyes, his mellow expression, the confidential inflection, let her know that everything was all right. Tension ebbed out of her like the remnants of a wave receding from shore. "Please."

He poured coffee for her and she took a seat at the table before her jellied knees gave way. The snap of his jeans rode an inch below his navel. The spot mesmerized her. Had her tongue actually been there, investigating in the dark? She ached with the need to touch him, to give him a good morning kiss that said thank you for a wonderful night—it was thrilling; I've never felt so feminine and desired.

"Would you like some breakfast?"

"Maybe just toast. I'm not very hungry."

"Neither am I."

For a moment that stretched out noticeably long, they stared at each other, transmitting a thousand and one silent, private messages. Eventually David asked Alicia a question and she roused herself enough to answer him. Pierce brought a plate of toast to the table and sat down across from her.

"You look pretty in that color of lavender."

The sweat suit was too nice to actually sweat in. "Thank you."

"Sleep well?"

His mouth was so beautiful. "Yes. You?"

"Dreams kept me from sleeping too soundly."

And that mouth had made her feel very beautiful. "I'm sorry."

He remembered all the times and all the places he had kissed her and his eyes dilated. "I didn't mind. They were good dreams."

"We're just like the people on the box, Mom."

Alicia dragged her eyes away from Pierce's and looked down at Adam. "I beg your pardon," she said vaguely.

"See." He pointed to the bright picture on the cereal box. "They're all sitting around the table eating breakfast. The two boys, that's me and David, and the mom and dad."

"That's not like us, stupid," David said. "Pierce can't be our dad. He would have to marry Mom first."

Adam's bottom lip stuck out belligerently. "Yeah, but then it'd be the same, wouldn't it, Mom?"

She didn't answer. She was too alarmed by the sudden paling of Pierce's face and the sexy cloudiness in his eyes being frozen out by hard, cold, brittle light. "Sort of the same. And, David, please don't call your brother stupid," she said distractedly. Her heart, which had been dancing joyously, now felt heavy. It was trying to sink into a vat of despair and she was holding onto it for dear life. "Why don't you two go outside and play if you're done?"

They were glad to be excused and headed for the door. "It'd be neat if Pierce was our dad, wouldn't it, David?"

"Yeah, we'd be just like the other kids and Chrissy could come see us and we could ride in the Porsche again."

"Gee. Would she be our sister or our aunt?"

"Our sister. Don't you know *anything*?"

"She sure is old to be a sister."

The screen door slammed behind them. Its loud banging only emphasized the ominous silence in the cabin.

Pierce set down his coffee mug. He did so with great care as though if he didn't, he would likely hurl it and its contents against the nearest wall. Sightlessly he stared into the cup. His jaw was as rigid as iron. In his temple, a vein ticked with pulsing blood. He swept his hair back with a raking gesture of tense fingers and then clenched them into a tight fist.

The transformation terrified Alicia. Not because she was afraid of him, but because she suspected what such a metamorphosis meant. "They're just little boys, Pierce." She couldn't help the pleading sound in her voice. "They don't realize the implications of what they said. They just know that our family isn't complete and the fact that they don't have a father bothers them. Please don't attach any special significance to what they said."

His smile was mirthless, frosty. "That sounds vaguely reminiscent of what we said to each other last night. But it *did* have 'special significance,' didn't it, Alicia?"

"I thought we'd already established that it did." She plucked at a loose thread. "Is that any reason to get angry?"

"Dammit, yes!" he shouted, vaulting out of the chair. Luckily the boys were yelling loudly at a squirrel and didn't hear him. Alicia did, however, and winced at his level of rage. "Yes, I'm angry."

"Why?" She recovered quickly. After last night, wasn't she entitled to know what his hang-ups were? "How can you get angry over a five-year-old boy mentioning marriage?"

"I'm not angry at Adam. My God, Alicia, give me some credit," he snapped. "I'm angry because last night was so damn good, because you are a woman I could fall very deeply in love with, because I want to be a father to your boys and make up for the mess I made of it the first time."

She gazed around her, waving her hands helplessly. "I don't understand you. Why is any of that bad?"

He grabbed her shoulders and shook her slightly. "Because none of it can happen." Each word was driven out of his mouth, holding on tenaciously, reluctant to be uttered.

He released her suddenly and she reeled. He turned his back and went to stare out the window, watching Adam and David as they picked up kindling wood and stacked it on top of the logs he had piled against the cabin the day before. He closed his eyes to the poignant sight and only wished he could close his ears to their conversation.

"This is the way Pierce taught us to do it."

"How come he knows so much stuff, David?"

"Because he's old, like a dad. Dads know lots of stuff."

"Do you think he'll be proud if we stack all this up?"

"Sure. He's always proud of us. Remember? He said so."

Alicia willed him to turn around and explain himself. When he didn't, she took the initiative. She was pushing and she knew it, but she wasn't about to leave him never knowing or understanding. "Why can't it happen?"

"Believe me, it can't."

"Why?"

"Drop it, please."

"Is there another woman?"

He turned toward her. His eyes swept her body and there was no disguising the desire that was still smoldering in them. "I wish it were that simple. To live with you, sleep with you every night, I'd give up any other woman I've ever met."

A small moan escaped her. "Then what is it, Pierce? Tell me."

"No."

"Why?"

"Because you're better off not knowing."

"Who made you the judge of that? After the intimacy we shared last night, can't we talk to each other openly and freely about anything?"

"Not about this."

"How could we possibly harbor secrets from each other after the way we've loved?"

"I didn't let myself think about it last night. This morning I *have* to think about it."

She laid her hands on her stomach, splayed wide. "I'm still carrying a living part of you inside me. But you can't confide in me? There's no logic in that."

The character lines were ironed out of his face as the skin stretched tightly across it. He stared at her hands where they pressed against her lower body. "My God," he strangled out. "You're on the pill, aren't you?"

"No."

His expletive was vicious and to the point. "Why didn't you tell me?"

"I don't recall your asking," she shot back. Her whole body was bristling with anger now. He had staggered away from her, but she reached for his arm and spun him around. "Don't worry, Mr. Reynolds. I'd never come begging after you with a baby on my arm."

"It's not that," he snarled. "I don't want to leave you pregnant, that's all."

"Leave me? This is it then?"

He drew in a deep sigh and his eyes softened considerably. "Yes. You knew that before you ever consented to stay the week here."

Yes. He had been honest about that. "I can't get involved," he had said. He had repeated it last night. She knew it, but she had ignored it. Their loving had been special, not just an exchange of flesh, but apparently Pierce Reynolds was stubbornly clinging to his reasons for not getting involved.

All right. To hell with him.

To save what scraps of pride she had left, she turned away from him and began to clear the table. Pierce went into the living room and finished dressing. When the dishes had been washed and neatly stacked—never let it be said that she and the boys had taken advantage of his hospitality—she went to him.

"I'm going back to L.A. this afternoon. It's a day earlier than I'd planned, but under the circumstances I think that's best." He was sitting on the couch, his hands folded between his wide spread knees, staring at the floor. "Pierce?" she said impatiently when he didn't respond. His head came up. He looked at her and nodded tersely.

On the verge of tears, she fled upstairs and began throwing things into their suitcases.

\*    \*    \*

Pierce stared after the car until it disappeared into the trees. The engulfing silence was cacophonous and hurt his ears.

*Go after them, you idiot. You damned fool.* How could he let them leave? He wanted the woman. He wanted the boys.

He didn't move because he knew he couldn't. In the long run it wouldn't be fair to any of them. He'd lived in a vacuum for almost a week. He'd remain there until he knew the answer one way or another. And either way it came out, he couldn't chance involving them.

He cursed his luck, cursed his life, and slammed the cabin door behind him as he entered its gloomy interior. He couldn't abide its shrouding depression. Shadows and sounds stalked him as he ranted through the small house. It would drive him mad to stay. He'd return to Los Angeles, too, just as soon as he could pack.


"It's your fault," David accused from the back seat. "He liked Adam and me but you made him mad. That's why we had to leave."

"We were going to leave tomorrow anyway." David and Adam were acting as though the Wicked Witch of the West was an angel compared to their mother. They had cried and whined and argued ever since she had virtually shoved them into the car and headed for home.

"Yeah, but tomorrow, not today."

"I didn't want to leave today either, David."

"Then why did we?"

Oh, God, she was tired of his harping on her. She craved peace, silence, solitude. She didn't want to make explanations because she had no explanations herself. Why couldn't she just go away someplace to lick her wounds, remember, savor, analyze, agonize? "Pierce wanted us to leave."

"Maybe he wanted you to, but he didn't want us to. He liked us."

"All right! That does it!" She drove the car off the highway and braked it to a teeth-jarring stop on the shoulder. Her face fierce with anger, she whirled around to face the boys. "I'm the bad guy. Okay, I've admitted it. Now shut up about Pierce and the cabin and the whole week. Got it? I don't want to hear any more about it."

Four eyes had gone wide and round with apprehension. Rarely did she lose her temper with them to that extent. "Say, 'Yes, ma'am,' " she instructed.

They responded tearfully, fearfully, their eyes watery and their lips wobbly. Her shoulders sagged. Everything inside her sagged. "Thank you."

She pulled back onto the highway and when she looked around several minutes later, both boys were asleep. David had a protective and comforting arm around Adam. Adam's thumb was in his mouth, something he hadn't done in a long time.

Alicia felt wretched for yelling at them, but her nerves were shot, her heart was broken, and she, more than anyone, felt like crying. Hours of hard sobbing sounded like a supreme luxury. She wanted to wallow in self-pity.

Why was she so unlucky in love? When would she learn to use some common sense, to practice caution, to beware? When would she grow up and stop being so gullible? Would she ever look beyond the surface of things? Why did she waltz blindly and foolishly into hopeless situations? Why had she had to fall in love with a man who wanted to race sports cars and get himself killed? Why had she thought herself in love with a man who liked, but obviously didn't love, her? Why now had she fallen in love—

The car nearly swerved off the road.

Had she fallen in love with Pierce?

Tears trekked from the corners of her eyes and rolled down her cheeks. Her bottom lip was pinched by bruising teeth. Her breasts heaved painfully.

Yes, she had. She was in love with Pierce. And a helluva lot of good it was going to do her.


"Good morning," Alicia greeted the saleswoman the following Monday morning as she pushed open the glass door and entered Glad Rags.

"Alicia! Hi. Have you heard the news since you got back?"

"I guess not. What news?"

"Gwen had her baby last Thursday night."

"Oh?" Alicia walked to the back of the shop, her footsteps soundless on the lush baby blue carpet. She hung her purse and jacket in the crowded employee's closet. The saleswoman had followed her.

"It was almost a month early, but weighed over six pounds. A little girl."

"How wonderful. How's Gwen?"

"Fine. Came through it like a charm."

"Good. I need to call her about the work that was done on her cabin."

"Can I get you some coffee?"

Alicia looked at her quizzically. "Awfully solicitous, aren't you? Is there something you're not telling me? Have I been fired in my absence?"

"Hardly." The woman lowered her voice. "The powers-that-be are in a meeting and asked me to send you in when you arrived. I think they want your decision today, Alicia."

"Hmm." Alicia accepted the coffee and took a sip. She hadn't expected it to come so soon, but she knew now what her answer would be. "Well, to the trenches." She winked at her cohort, checked out her appearance in the hall mirror, and took the stairs to the chain's executive offices on the second floor.

"Hello, Alicia, they're expecting you. Go right in," the owners' secretary said with all the cordiality of an undertaker.

"Thank you."

Summoning all her poise, Alicia opened the heavy oak door and entered the inner sanctum. She was greeted by a cloud of cigar smoke and hearty hellos.

After being politely seated, offered coffee, and queried about her week of vacation, they put the important question to her.

She had almost blown it again. She had almost let herself slip into that old habit of dependency on someone else for her happiness. She had two wonderful sons, two healthy legs to stand on, a keen mind, and creative ideas. After several hours of hard weeping, more hours of cursing and stomping, and two days of soul searching, she had decided she didn't need Pierce Reynolds. She didn't need anything except her own ingenuity.

"My time and talents are expensive," she told them bluntly. "I want three hundred dollars a month more than you offered."

They conferred and met her terms.

"Well, sirs, you have yourself a new Fashion Coordinator. Shall I outline some of my ideas?"

Her smiling enthusiasm captivated them.


"I love it," she said, knocking on the plate glass window. The window dresser turned around and gave her the thumbs-up sign. She pushed through the door.

"Thanks for the idea. I think it looks terrific."

"It does," she said, glad that her idea of featuring belts

in the window had sparked such a creative response in him.

"You look terrific too."

Because of her promotion and the hefty increase in salary she had splurged on the outfit. The skirt was a long swirl of lightweight ivory wool. The blouse she wore with it was teal silk. She had slung a fringed paisley print shawl over one shoulder and belted it at her waist with one of the designer belts she was featuring in the window. Pale stockings and bone pumps completed the businesslike, but softly feminine, ensemble.

She curtsied. "From our Beverly Hills store."

He whistled long and low. "Wrap them up. I'll take a dozen. If the girl comes with them, that is."

She tilted her head to one side and put her hands on her hips. "What would your boyfriend say?"

He grinned at her. "We're open-minded. He'd be delighted to have a lady like you join us one night."

She laughed and shook her head. "I'm afraid I'm not quite that open-minded."

"I was afraid this was going to happen." He sighed theatrically. "One week with a new title and she's too prickly to have a good time with us commoners."

Alicia swatted a hand at him and went to answer the ringing telephone. She could see that the two saleswomen were with customers.

"Glad Rags."

"Is Mrs. Alicia Russell there, please?"

"This is Alicia Russell."

"Mrs. Russell, this is Westbrook Clinic calling. We have your son here."

All the air rushed out of her body at once and she slumped against the counter. "My son? At the hospital?"

"David. He had an accident at school. The principal brought him in."

"Is he—"

"He's fine, but he's crying for you. Can you come right away? I'm afraid we need you to sign—"

"Oh God, yes. I'm on my way."

She slammed the phone down and, picking up her purse again, raced for the door. "David's been taken to the hospital," she called over her shoulder to the saleswoman who had noticed the nature of the call and was standing nearby. "I'll probably be gone the rest of the day."

"Is it serious? Do you want someone with you?"

"I don't think so. I don't know. No. I don't want anybody with me."

The California sunshine struck her eyes like a laser, but she didn't take time to put on her sunglasses. Her hands were shaking uncontrollably as she tried to unlock the door of her car. Traffic was snarled on the avenues and sluggish on the freeways. Her eyes were tearless, but her throat was clogged with the need to cry.

Was it a broken bone? A scratch? What? Why hadn't she asked? Was he bleeding? And where the hell was Westbrook Clinic? Oh, yes, on Montgomery Street near the boys' school. Thirty minutes from here.

When at last the clinic came into sight, she screeched the car to a stop and dashed for the entrance. Automatic doors slid open and she ran through them. "David Russell," she said breathlessly to the nurse behind the reception desk.

"Are you Mrs. Russell?"

"Yes, how is he? I got here as quickly as I could." She could easily have slapped the nurse for her cool, calm efficiency and the slightly reproachful curl of her thin lips.

"He's in treatment room five down this corridor. I'll bring the papers in for you to sign before we can treat him."

She wanted to ask if they'd let a child die because some damned form hadn't been signed, but she didn't want to waste her breath or her time. She ran down the corridor, her heels striking hollows thuds that matched her heartbeats.

She heard his whimpers of pain even before she reached the door and pushed it open. The first sight that greeted her was a blood-saturated towel lying on the floor. Nausea gushed to her throat. "David?" A man was bending over him. He straightened and turned around. It was Pierce.

# *Six*

"What are you doing here?"

"David had them call me."

"Mommy?"

The pitiful, frightened cry superseded her shock over seeing Pierce. Rushing to the side of the examination table, she looked down at her son and barely stifled a gasp. His right eye was almost swollen shut. An inch-long gash had been cut from the middle of his eyebrow to well past the outer corner. It had stopped bleeding, but the raw flesh lay open . . . obscenely open.

"David, baby, what happened? Oh, Lord! Are you in pain?"

"It hurts, Mommy." Blindly he groped for her, catching a fistful of her shawl.

"I know, I know it hurts, sweetheart." Frantically she looked up at Pierce. "Have they done anything for him? What about his eye?"

He shook his head. "They wouldn't let me sign the permission for treatment. He can see out of his eye. I already tested him on it."

"Thank God," she breathed as she gripped David's hand. "We're going to get you fixed up. I promise."

"Don't leave me, Mommy," he cried when she began to draw her hand from his.

"I'm not going to leave you. I'm only going to get the doctor."

Just then the nurse swished in crisply. "Mrs. Russell, if you'll please sign this form and give me the name of your insurance company and your policy number, I can give David a shot to relieve his pain."

"I don't want a shot," David screamed and began to cry.

"Hey, hey, what was that promise we made each other about being brave? Hmm?" Pierce lay a consoling hand on the boy's shoulder and bent over him.

Alicia fumbled in her handbag for her wallet where she kept her insurance cards. When the forms had been properly filled out, the nurse prepared a syringe with a mild sedative. "It won't hurt so bad in his hip."

Alicia and Pierce, working together, got David's belt unbuckled, turned him over, and lowered his jeans. He was crying copiously. Alicia's heart was wrenching.

"Now we'll let that take effect while we wait for Dr. Benedict," the nurse said.

"What do you mean wait?" Alicia demanded heatedly. "I want my son seen to immediately. What's wrong with you people?"

"Alicia, I took the liberty of calling Frank Benedict," Pierce said calmly. "He's a plastic surgeon, a friend of mine. I thought you might want a plastic surgeon to suture David since the cut is in such a visible place on his face."

"Oh," she said in a small voice. "Of course. I probably would have done that myself. Thank you, Pierce."

The nurse looked at her smugly as she went out the door. No doubt she had assessed Alicia as an unfit mother who couldn't be found when her son was injured. She had assumed Pierce was her lover.

Wasn't he?

The staff doctor, looking alarmingly young and breezy, bustled through the door. He was wearing jeans and jogging shoes with his laboratory coat. "Hi. Which one of you is David? No, let me guess. You," he said, pointing to the boy, "the one with the busted eye. What did you run into, buddy?" He coaxed a shaky smile from the patient.

In a nonchalant and what seemed to Alicia unsympathetic-to-pain manner, he swabbed the cut with antiseptic. When his fingers separated the lips of the wound and she saw the depth of it, nausea surged burningly into her throat again and she slumped against the wall. Strobe lights went off behind her eyelids. Had it not been for a pair of strong arms suddenly supporting her, she would have collapsed to the floor when her knees gave way to rubbery weakness.

"Hang in there. David's going to be all right."

God, his voice sounded wonderful. How had she lived for a whole week without hearing it? His hands felt good, strong, sure, safe. She leaned against him. His body was warm, tough, and solid, able to ward off the worst of nightmares. She allowed herself only a precious moment of actually touching him, then she straightened.

"David had you notified?" she asked, tilting her head up to look at him.

He nodded. "When you couldn't be located, he gave them my name and the name of the company."

"I must have been in transit between stores."

"Don't blame yourself. You can't be expected to sit by a telephone all day long. As soon as I spoke with the principal of the school and he told me what had happened, I rushed right over."

"Thank you. I'm sorry."

"Sorry?" He frowned. "For what?"

"For your being . . . called, involved in this."

He scowled and looked away from her for a moment. She could almost hear him mentally swearing. When his eyes came back to her they were seething with anger.

Taking the coward's way out, she avoided the issue. "I—I still don't know what happened."

"It was just after recess. The kids were being rowdy. Someone slung open the classroom door and David caught it with his eye."

She covered her mouth with her hand. Her fingers were cold, unworkable, stiff. They were clasped and warmly chafed. Pierce rubbed heat and life back into them. "He'll be fine. I know it," he whispered. His flare of temper had disappeared as quickly as it had come.

"Naw, the Cowboys don't stand a chance against the Rams' defensive line," the doctor was saying to David.

"They're pretty good."

The doctor snorted derisively. "Not a chance. I'd lay money on it. There, all done. Clean as a whistle. That fancy stitchin' doc will have you lookin' good in no time."

He sailed out and they were left alone.

Alicia leaned over David and brushed back strands of his hair from the pale, clammy forehead. How vulnerable he looked lying on that sterile table. She hated it.

The shot was taking effect and he was drowsy. "Mommy, I got blood on Miss Thompkins's blouse. Do you think she's gonna be mad at me?"

Tears trickled down Alicia's cheeks, but she smiled. "I don't think so. If she is, I'll buy her a new one."

"I'm sorry you had to leave work."

"No job is as important to me as you are."

"Is this the first time I've been in the hospital?"

"Except for when you were born."

"Daddy was there then."

"Yes, he was."

"I'm glad Pierce is here this time. Aren't you, Mommy?"

Alicia's eyes sought out his. He was holding David's hand and rubbing the knuckles with his thumb. He lifted his head and looked at her across the table and she knew how much she had been missed. His eyes told her so.

"Yes, I'm very glad Pierce is here."

The door was pushed open. "Pierce?"

"Hi, Frank." The two men shook hands. "This is Alicia Russell and her son David, friends of mine."

"Hello," the doctor said cordially. He was a man about Pierce's age, shorter, balding, and paunchy.

"David had an altercation with a door and the door won."

Dr. Benedict peered down at David's eye. Now that the banalities were out of the way, he was all business. "I'll say it did." He patted the boy on the knee. "I'm going to give that cut some medicine to put it to sleep."

"Shots?" David asked tremulously.

"Little tiny ones that you won't even feel. Then I'm going to sew you up with a needle and thread. Do you know what silk is?"

"Like Mommy's blouses?"

"Yeah. Only the thread I'll use is even softer than her blouses."

"Gee."

The doctor began rolling up his shirtsleeves to wash his hands. He turned to Alicia and Pierce who had moved aside while he was examining David. "Why don't you wait outside?"

"But—" Alicia began to protest.

"It'll be easier, Mrs. Russell, I assure you. Wait outside."

She looked imploringly at Pierce, but he nodded agreement with the doctor. She took David's hand and squeezed it. "When I see you again, it'll all be over." She kissed his forehead and let herself be led out the door as the nurse came through carrying a tray of medical implements.

"Will he be okay?" Her question was as anxious as the hand clutching his sleeve.

"Frank's great with kids. He has four of his own."

"David looked so little, so helpless, lying there."

"I know. It scared hell out of me too when I first saw him."

They heard David cry out sharply and then sob painfully.

Alicia rushed toward the door, but Pierce detained her with a steady arm across her shoulders. "It's all right. He's okay. You know that." He leaned back against the wall and pulled her into his arms, pressing her head down onto his chest. "Shhh, it's okay," he repeated in comforting whispers. His body absorbed her trembling as she wept.

David wasn't crying any longer. They could hear the doctor talking to him in muted tones. The words were indistinct, but the inflection was lulling.

Alicia's own distress subsided beneath the healing power of Pierce's touch. His fingers sifted through her hair, massaging her scalp. His other hand soothingly rubbed her back. "You look beautiful today. I've never seen you dressed up."

She laughed against his starched shirt front. "I was hardly *haute couture* at the cabin, was I?"

"I like you both ways."

"Do you?" Her words were barely audible.

"Yes."

"I've never seen you in a jacket and tie either."

"And?"

She raised her head. His was the most perfectly masculine face she had ever seen. Not as handsome as some, not even as classically handsome as her dark and dashing Jim had been, but the features were so arrestingly arranged; the man was so sensuously appealing. Even dressed for business as he was, his hair was still styled casually. His face bore the marks of the wind and rain and sun from his week in the woods. His cologne was painfully familiar and stabbed her lungs with memories each time she inhaled.

She wanted to tell him that she didn't care how he was dressed, he always looked good to her. She wanted to say that she was so glad to see *him*, she had barely noticed what he was wearing.

But she didn't say anything because she didn't know what his being here might mean and because she was worried about her son. So rather than having to think up something appropriate to say, she simply settled against him again and basked in the feel of his arms around her.

For right now, she needed him and he was here. It might turn out to be a foolish indulgence, but she wasn't going to deny herself his comforting.

Twenty minutes later, the nurse summoned them at Dr. Benedict's request. "His eye is fine," he said to Alicia immediately as she entered the treatment room. She flew to David's side and took his hand. His right eye was covered by a white gauze bandage. "If he complains of blurred vision or anything out of the ordinary, you should have an ophthalmologist check it, but I don't anticipate any trouble. I don't think he'll have much of a scar, but we'll monitor the healing process closely."

"Hi, Mom. Can I wear the bandage to school tomorrow?"

Dr. Benedict laughed. "Let's give it a few days, David, until the swelling goes down."

"How many stitches did you say I got?"

"Only seven on the outside, but a whole lot more underneath. You be sure and tell the other kids that."

"Okay!" David beamed.

The doctor went over treatment of the incision with Alicia and gave her a prescription for an antibiotic. "Thanks, Frank, for coming so soon," Pierce said.

"No problem. You'll get my bill," he said jovially.

"No. Send the bill to me," Alicia said. Both men looked at her, stunned. She hadn't intended her words to sound so emphatic and waspish, but that's the way they had come out.

"Yes, well, of course," the doctor blustered. "Good-bye, David. I'll see you in a week to take out the stitches. Call the office for an appointment," he said to Alicia.

"I will. Thank you." She was embarrassed and wondered what the doctor thought her relationship with Pierce was. What *was* her relationship with Pierce?

David insisted on walking, though Pierce offered to carry him to the car. He was woozier than he thought and they supported him between them until they reached the parking lot.

"Pierce, thank you so much for coming—"

"I'm driving you home."

"That isn't necessary."

He gnawed on his bottom lip in vexation. "Here, David, get in and lie down." He opened the back door of her car and helped the boy in. Then he shut the door and, turning, stormed toward Alicia, grabbed her arm, and dragged her out of hearing distance.

"Will you stop being so damned defensive? Frank was making a joke about his bill."

"I know that," she said, freeing her arm with a vicious tug. "I spouted off before I realized it. I'm sorry if I embarrassed you in front of your friend. But I didn't want him to think that I was . . . was . . ."

"Well?" he demanded impatiently. "What didn't you want him to think?"

"That I was a kept woman who depended on you to pay my bills. A mistress."

"Oh, come on," he cried. "What history book did you dredge up that word from?"

"You know what I mean."

"Yes, I know what you mean." He ran his hand through his hair. "You can't stop people from jumping to conclusions, so don't worry about what they think. We know we're not involved that way."

"That's right. We do," she said furiously. "God knows I've heard it often enough from you. So what are you doing here? Do you blame me for being defensive? You with your sexy bedroom eyes across the breakfast table one minute and your accusations that I might trap you by getting pregnant the next."

"I never made any such accusation," he growled.

"Didn't you?"

"I was concerned for you, not for me."

"I think I heard that line on a soap opera once."

"It's the truth."

"So that's what this is about? *Concern* for the little widow and her two children?"

"Yes. Partially."

"You rushed over here today, disrupted my life again out of human compassion, benevolence, Christian charity?"

"Whatever you want to call it."

She wanted to call it love, but didn't have the nerve. She wanted to fling the word in his face just to see how he would react. Instead they stared at each other across the space that separated them, breathing heavily, each feeling a little ridiculous about this argument taking place on a public parking lot.

Finally Pierce stepped forward and curled his fingers

around her upper arm. She knew it would be useless to try to free them this time. "You're in no condition to drive. I'm taking you and David home and you can read whatever you like into it."

She surrendered because she didn't feel like fighting with him any more. But mostly because, for whatever his reasons, she wanted him to come home with her.

*Spineless, stupid female,* she silently berated herself. But she meekly followed him. He seated her in the passenger side of her car. "What about your car?"

"I'll pick it up later. Let me lock it up."

It was low, foreign, lean, and mean. It was like the cars the long, leggy girls climb out of in pantyhose and perfume commercials, trailing skeins of hair and yards of mink behind them. And it perfectly suited the man. Alicia wondered how many leggy women had climbed out of that car under Pierce's escort. Frank Benedict hadn't seemed surprised to find his friend taking care of a woman. Probably he had seen Pierce in that role many times before.

He slid beneath the steering wheel. "How's the patient?"

"He's fallen asleep."

"Still dopey, I guess. What about Adam?"

Alicia consulted her watch and was dismayed to see how late in the afternoon it was. "He'll already be home with the after-school sitter. I hope David's car pool driver heard what happened to him."

"The principal said he'd take care of it."

That was a worry that hadn't even occurred to Alicia. What had the boys' elementary school principal thought of Pierce when he showed up at the clinic? What had David told him about Pierce? "D-did you meet Mr. Jenkins?"

"Yes." He could read her like a book, or so his wry grin told her. "I told him I was an old friend of the family's."

"Oh."

Adam was suitably and jealously impressed with David's bandage, the plastic hospital wristband with his name written on it, and all the attention his older brother was getting. Once David was changed into pajamas and in bed, Pierce invited Adam to drive with him to the drugstore to pick up David's prescription. That appeased his sense of fair play. When they came back, his arms were full of comic books and small board games.

"Me and Pierce bought them for you," Adam said, dumping the prizes onto the bed.

"And a new game cartridge for your Atari," Pierce added.

"It's busted," David said dismally.

"Oh?" Pierce squatted down in front of the video unit. "Maybe I can fix it."

Alicia groaned. While he was on the errand, she had telephoned her parents about David's accident and they were on their way over. She had hoped Pierce would be gone by the time they arrived. No such luck. They came to the door with Jim's parents in tow and both sets of grandparents swarmed into the sickroom in time to see Pierce sitting with Adam in the middle of the floor, the entrails of the video equipment strewn around them, and a seemingly recovered David peering over his shoulder and offering advice.

"Such a nice man," Alicia's mother commented with studied indifference. Someone had gone out for fried chicken. After the indoor picnic, Alicia's mother had insisted that she help clean up. Alicia just wanted everybody to go home. Her head was pounding and she imagined her nerves to look like the frazzled ends of overpermed hair.

"Who?"

"Alicia, how many men do you have repairing your television sets and replacing unreachable light bulbs?"

"Oh, Pierce. Yes, he is nice."

"Have you known him long? I'm surprised that David would call him before he'd call us."

She hadn't told her parents about their week in Pierce's cabin. When they had asked about the vacation, she had simply told them that she and the boys had enjoyed a very good time and thanked her lucky stars that David and Adam hadn't been around to fill in the details. Some things a girl, no matter how old, never told her mother. "I haven't known him too long," she replied evasively, "but the boys like him."

"He's older than most of the men you've dated."

"We're not dating. Exactly."

Exactly what were they doing? She couldn't be accused of sleeping with him on their first date. They hadn't had a first date.

By the time the grandparents left and David and Adam were settled for the night, Alicia felt like collapsing in a heap and never getting up. "Here, drink this," Pierce said, handing her a glass.

"What is it?"

"I'm not sure," he said with a twisted smile. "Your supply of spirits is limited, to say the least. I had to search until I found this labelless bottle in the top shelf of the kitchen pantry."

"I think it's the brandy I used to pour over a Christmas fruit cake."

"Drink up." He tilted the glass toward her lips. She sipped and sputtered on the fiery liquor. Pierce set the glass on the coffee table. Laughing softly, he lifted amber droplets from her lips with the tip of his finger. Their eyes locked, his laughter subsided, and they became very still.

He painted her lips with the brandy on the tip of his

finger. His eyes dropped to her mouth that waited soft and moist and fragrant with the bouquet of the liquor. His tongue tasted it first as it flicked lightly over her lips. "Whatever it is, it's delicious," he whispered.

"Is it?"

"This way it is." His arms closed around her. Her lips needed no persuasion to open beneath his. They did so willingly, sacrificially, and took his tongue deep inside. The kiss was long and thorough, heady with emotion, intoxicating. When they at last surfaced for air, they were both dizzy and clung to each other.

Pierce lay his lips against her ear. "Your bath water is getting cold."

"My what?" Her voice sounded like a cello string that had been plucked and didn't know whether to vibrate or not. She didn't want to move. She wanted to stay molded against him for the rest of her life. "My bath?"

He disengaged them. "While you were saying good-bye to your folks I drew you a hot bath. Come on."

Taking her hand, he led her into her bedroom. She looked around it as though expecting it to have undergone a change since he'd been in it. It was remarkably the same. Her bathroom was steamy from a scented bubble bath in the deep tub.

"That looks heavenly." She sighed.

"Take your time. I'll run interference, answer the phone, that kind of thing. And," he said, laying his finger across lips that had started to speak, "if anyone should call, I'll identify myself as a cousin or brother or something."

"I don't have a brother."

He kissed the tip of her nose. "Take your bath." The door closed behind him.

When she emerged from her bedroom she was wrapped in a blue silk kimono and a haze of sexual excitement. "Any word out of the boys?" she asked softly.

Pierce was sitting on the living room sofa watching television. At the sound of her voice he switched off the set and stood to face her. His eyes went wide with appreciation, then narrow with hunger. "No. I just checked on them. They're both sleeping."

She rustled into the room, trying to act normal, trying to pretend that her thighs weren't melting and her insides weren't churning. With feigned negligence, she pinched a dead leaf off one of her plants. "I like your house," Pierce said, his voice rough.

"Thank you." Stucco walls, Italian tile floors, shutters on the windows. Her house was as it had been since she bought it soon after Jim's death. But suddenly everything around her seemed alien. She felt that the only place she would ever feel at home was in Pierce's arms. The notion was absurd—but stimulating. "I want to do some redecorating, buy new furniture, but I'm going to wait until the boys are older."

"That's probably smart."

They were talking about nothing, playing at conversation, pretending this was a casual encounter between old friends and not an electrically charged rendezvous between lovers.

Pierce was cursing himself. Why was he standing here talking like an idiot when what he wanted to be doing was holding her, caressing her, kissing her? Was she really naked beneath her robe or was that just a depraved hope of his warped mind?

"What about work?" he asked. She was naked. Faintly visible through the soft fabric were the dusky areolas and the sweet impudence of her nipples.

"I called them and said I wouldn't be in tomorrow." He looked rakishly attractive with his shirtsleeves rolled up. His jacket and tie were draped over the back of a chair.

Three buttons on his shirt were undone. She wanted to rip the rest open, to see all of his chest and not just that inviting wedge with its forest of soft, crinkly hair.

"I mean about your decision."

"I accepted the job." Her smile was confident, proud, and he smiled with her.

"That's great. Do you like it?"

She tossed back her hair and said a trifle breathlessly, "It's a challenge." His eyes were burning the kimono off her body. She could feel their heat as they toured her. Why didn't he come to her and embrace her? "I've never been so busy. I'm going to New York next spring to buy the fall lines."

"You'll do a good job." God, he wanted her. He needed her.

"I hope so."

"I'm sure of it."

"Thank you for the vote of confidence."

She felt anything but confident. It had been so long since she had entertained a man. How did one go about it? Was he waiting for her to make the first move? Did he think that after their argument of this afternoon she didn't want him? Couldn't he tell that she was dying to be loved? She took a step toward him.

"Would you like some—What's that?" An automobile horn was honking outside.

He took a long time answering. "A cab," he finally stated in a flat, dead tone. "I called for one while you were in the bathroom. I can't stay. I have to go, Alicia."

She glanced at the door, then back at him, disbelief replacing her expectant expression of a moment ago. His eyes pleaded for understanding, but as he watched, her face stiffened into an expressionless mask. "Of course," she said tightly. "Thank you for everything."

"Don't, please."

"Don't what?"

"Don't get angry and make it harder for me to leave than it already is."

She laughed harshly. "I don't know why you find it hard. You've had so much practice at it."

The horn honked imperiously. Pierce jerked open the front door and shouted, "I'll be right there."

"I ain't waitin' for free, mister."

"So start your meter."

He slammed the door closed and advanced into the room. "I must go. If I stay—"

"So go!" she shouted.

"If I stay, I'll make love to you."

"God forbid."

"And I'll spend the night, making love to you all night."

"And you don't want to get involved," she mocked.

"It's impossible."

"I understand."

"You don't."

"Explain it to me then."

"I can't."

"Oh, damn you!" she cried and turned her back on him. Immediately she spun around again, her eyes afire with anger. "Why did you even bother, Pierce? Why didn't you just act like you'd never heard of David Russell when they called from the school? Why did you come home with us? Why any of it, Pierce? *Why?*"

Three long strides brought him to her and he closed hard fingers around her upper arms and pulled her to him. "Because I care. Because I adore your sons and wish like hell they were mine. And because I want you so bad I can't do anything without seeing you, feeling you, tasting—"

An anguished sound was torn from his throat just a heartbeat before his mouth fused with hers. He kissed her fiercely, his tongue plowing deep with undisciplined passion. Her head fell back over the arm supporting her shoulders. His lips only followed to plunder her neck and throat before taking her mouth again.

His hand pushed aside the robe and found her breast. He kneaded it possessively. Her nipple pearled beneath the finessing of his thumb and they both shuddered under the impact of inundating desire.

His mouth tempered its lust slightly as it continued to ravage her mouth, but sweetly, so sweetly. Her fingers tunneled through his hair. Anger had only given her passions impetus. She was wild with her need for him. All the trauma of the day reared up to become unbridled desire. Her body arched against his, straining for fulfillment. She reached for him. Touched him.

He swore savagely. He prayed. He rubbed himself against her hand. "I want you," he whispered raggedly. "I want you, your mouth, your breasts." The words tripped fervently from his busy lips. He clasped her to him as though he would never let her go and planted his mouth in the hollow of her neck. "Can't you feel how much I want you? Do you think I've forgotten how it feels to be inside you? Do you know what it's doing to me to leave you now?" He cupped his hands around her face and dragged his thumbs over her kiss-swollen lips. "I want you, my darling, but I can't have you."

And with that, he was gone and she was alone.


The days passed in a grueling, hectic routine that should have exhausted her enough to sleep every night through without waking. But Alicia was plagued by insomnia. She was prone to weep every night at bedtime, hugging her pillow to her and wishing for Pierce's strong warmth, his ardent kisses, his erotic caresses.

In the daytime, two emotions warred within her. She was furious with him. She hated him. How dare he do this to her again? It was cruel beyond measure to torment her this way. But he wasn't a cruel man. So what game was he playing? Or was it a game? Would she ever see him again? And that's when the second emotion would set in. That's when a black, fathomless loneliness would enclose her and she was powerless to fight her way out of it.

She could easily murder him for what he had done to her—twice. But on the other hand she was constantly looking over her shoulder in the hope of seeing him.

That's why, when the doorbell rang on the evening of the day David had his stitches taken out, she jumped reflexively and her breath and pulse rate accelerated madly. Was it he? Was he coming by to check on David? Was he coming to beg her forgiveness?

Wetting her lips and combing trembling hands through her hair, she went to the door. She took a deep breath and pulled it open.

"Oh my God, what's happened?" was her startled cry.

# Seven

"Is Daddy here?"

Chrissy Reynolds's eye makeup had bled down her cheeks on what must have been a torrent of tears that wasn't yet checked. Her expensive dinner dress was wilted and wrinkled, her stockings had a run. A well-maintained short hairdo had gone haywire.

"Chrissy, what in the world?" Alicia exclaimed, pulling the girl through the door. Thank heaven the boys were already asleep. They would have been frightened to see Pierce's daughter in such a state. "What's happened to you?" Had she been attacked?

"Daddy's not here?" she wailed.

"No." Alicia led her to the sofa and she sank down on the cushions, burying her face in her hands.

"I thought he might be here. I've been calling his house, but there was no answer. I looked up your number in the phone book at a telephone booth and realized I was so close that I came by rather than calling. I have to see Daddy. Do you know where he is?"

"No, I haven't heard from him in a week. David hurt his eye and—"

"Oh, I'm sorry, Alicia. Daddy told me about that. How is David?"

Pierce had told her? He hadn't called, though he had sent David a different card every day. "He's fine, but what's happened to you?"

Chrissy's snorting laugh lacked humor. She sniffed back tears. "I created a scene at the party tonight. It was held in honor of my fiancé and me. Only he's not my fiancé anymore."

Alicia took Chrissy's hand and said calmly, "Tell me."

The distraught young woman seemed only too glad to have a sympathetic ear. "Oh Alicia, I don't know what happened to me. Just suddenly there were too many false people, wearing too many false smiles, offering us empty wishes with trite phrases. I looked at my fiancé, and wondered what in the hell I was doing there with him then and what I was going to do with him the rest of our lives." She laughed again. "I said, 'Do you love me?' And he stared at me as though I'd lost my mind. I took off my engagement ring, handed it back to him, and made the announcement over the bandleader's microphone that the wedding was off."

Alicia covered her laugh with her hand. "You didn't."

"I did."

"I'm sorry, I don't mean to laugh, but I can just visualize the stir that must have caused."

"I thought Mother was going to have a stroke."

"Wasn't your father there?"

"Earlier, but he had left. That's why I thought he might be here. He didn't have a date tonight and seemed in a hurry to get away. Mother, of course, was furious with him for leaving right after dinner."

Alicia wanted to pursue the reason Pierce didn't have a date. The way Chrissy had said it led her to believe that his behavior tonight was quite a departure from the norm. She, too, wondered where he was at this hour. Maybe he had a late date with a woman unsuitable to attend his daughter's engagement party. The thought gave her such pain that she thrust it aside.

"What are you going to do?" she asked Chrissy.

Heaving a sigh, Chrissy reclined against the cushions of the sofa and let her head drop. "Beyond the moment, I don't know."

"Well then, let's concentrate on the moment," Alicia said cheerfully. "I don't think you need to be driving around the streets of Los Angeles this late at night as upset as you are. Why don't you take a hot bath and spend the night here?"

"I couldn't impose on you that way."

Alicia could tell that, despite her protest, the idea appealed to Chrissy. She looked emotionally and physically exhausted. "It's not an imposition. The boys will be thrilled to find you here in the morning."

Chrissy smiled, but then she groaned. "I can't stay, Alicia. Mother will have the FBI out looking for me. She'll call Daddy and get him upset. And I really want to talk to him."

"I'll keep trying to reach him." The girl would never know how much it cost Alicia to offer that service. "Let's get you out of that dress," she said, standing. "I'll find something for you to sleep in." Pierce had offered to do that for her at the cabin. A vision of the black nightgown he had found came to her mind. He had held it up to her, his eyes had . . .

Chrissy was ensconced in the guest room and Alicia checked to see that it was stocked with everything she would need. She tapped on the bathroom door. "Everything all right? Feeling better?"

"This is just what I needed. Thanks so much, Alicia."

"I'm glad to have you." She paused. "Uh, Chrissy,

what is your father's telephone number? I'll try to call him for you."

Chrissy told her and during the next several minutes she dialed it twice. There was no answer. Chrissy joined her in the kitchen where she was sipping a cup of herbal tea. She had put on her nightclothes. Chrissy was wrapped in a borrowed robe.

Chrissy stirred honey into her tea after Alicia set it in front of her. She took a tentative sip. The contents of the cup seemed to intrigue her. She stared into it for several long moments. "Alicia," she said hesitantly, "it's none of my business, I know, but how is it that you didn't even know Daddy's home telephone number?"

Idly Alicia stirred her own tea. "I've never had occasion to call him."

"Then I was wrong? There was nothing going on between the two of you that week at the cabin?"

"Your father is a very attractive man," Alicia said, squirming uneasily in her chair.

"But not your type?"

Exactly her type. If one was a woman, Pierce was her type. "He's probably not accustomed to romancing a woman with two active little boys tagging along."

"He's crazy about your kids. He told me so." She sipped her tea and watched Alicia over the cup. "He's crazy about you too."

"H-how do you know?" She tried to act disinterested. She failed. Chrissy's eyes were pure mischief.

"I asked him if he got lucky and scored with you." Alicia's shocked face made her laugh. "No, I didn't. At least not in those words."

"What did he say?"

"Oh, he carried on for a full five minutes about how you were intelligent and fun and charming and beautiful and a good mother and a good listener and lovely and soft and feminine. So I said, 'Well?' and he said, 'There are problems.' "

"Oh."

"What problems? Are you still hung up on your husband or something?"

"No."

"Then I don't get it. Daddy's always been a ladies' man. I hope you don't mind my saying that."

"That would be obvious to anyone."

"So, what problems? Any woman he's ever been attracted to, he went after and usually got. If she weren't so inclined, his attitude was to hell with it."

Alicia was shaking her head. "I don't see your point."

Chrissy laid her hands flat on the table and leaned over to stress her meaning. "Look, I'm not blind. You two couldn't wait to jump on each other's bones. Now whether you did or not, I don't know. But whatever's happened, you're both walking wrecks now. Daddy looked like pure hell tonight, and when I asked him why, he said he wasn't sleeping well. And frankly, you don't look so great either. So what's with you two? If you're that hot for each other, what have you got to lose?"

Alicia could have asked that of Pierce herself. "There are problems," she repeated softly, sadly.

"Well," Chrissy sighed and stood up, "who am I to give advice to the lovelorn? I have just jilted one of the most sought-after bachelors in southern California." They laughed, but each was lost in her own thoughts. "I'm off to bed, if you don't mind."

"Of course not."

"If you're going to be up for a while, will you keep trying Daddy? I could call Mother and tell her where I am, but I don't want to cope with one of her tirades right now. Do you understand?"

"I understand." Alicia smiled kindly. "Good night."

Chrissy leaned down and kissed her cheek. " 'Night. Thanks, Alicia, for everything."


It was only an hour before dawn when he answered the telephone. Alicia had called every half hour. She told herself that her diligence was for Chrissy's sake and that she wasn't able to sleep anyway. The real reason was that she was worried about Pierce herself. Or was that, too, a rationalization? Was she driven by jealousy to know where he could be at that time of night and with whom? Anyway she kept dialing until he answered with a brusque, "Yes?"

"Pierce?" His abrupt, anxious tone had caught her off guard.

"Yes, this is Pierce Reynolds. Who is this?"

"Alicia."

"Alicia!" he exclaimed. She could almost visualize him checking his watch for the time. "Is something wrong?"

"No, I—"

"Then can I call you back? I'm trying to keep the line clear. Something's happened to Chrissy."

"She's here."

"Where?"

"Here. At my house."

Pierce sank onto his bed and let his head drop forward as his shoulders slumped in relief. "Is she all right?"

"She's fine, though she was terribly upset when she arrived."

"When was that?"

"About midnight. I've been trying to reach you since then."

He heard the question in her voice. Did she think he'd been out with another woman? If only he could tell her he'd been trying very hard to get very drunk. It hadn't worked. Even alcohol couldn't dull his memories of her nor dilute the ghost of her that danced in front of his eyes just out of reach.

Finally, he'd gone to an all-night coffee shop and eaten breakfast. He hadn't been able to push a bite past his throat at the fancy dinner Dottie had thrown in honor of Chrissy and her young man. It had been more to honor Dottie for making a good match. The whole thing had sickened him.

"I've been out."

"Oh."

God, he wished he could tell her how much he missed her. "I guess Chrissy told you what she did at the party. Her mother called here just as I was coming in about fifteen minutes ago. She was hysterical, but that's not unusual for Dottie."

"Chrissy wanted desperately to talk to you, but otherwise she was okay." She paused, knowing it wasn't her place to ask. "Pierce, you're not angry with her, are you?"

"Hell, no. I'm glad she's out of it."

Alicia was relieved. She knew Chrissy would be devastated if her father censured the daring action she'd taken. "Good. She's so anxious to talk to you. She needs to know you'll stand behind her decision."

"She's got my endorsement. Should I come over?"

"She's sleeping now."

*But you're not,* Pierce was thinking. *And I'm not. And I'd love to be holding you. Lying in bed, holding each other close until the sun came up.* "Then I'll wait till morning."

"It is morning."

Was there reproach in her voice? "Later in the morning."

"All right. I'll tell her you'll be over about nine, say?"

"Fine. Good night."

"Good night."

Not good night, my love. Not good night, darling. Not even good night, Pierce. Just good night. She was put out with him. And he didn't blame her one bit. He had been a bastard. If only she knew he had had to be one for her own good.

He got there at eighty-thirty. He hadn't been able to sleep so he had showered, shaved, dressed, and killed time until he thought he could arrive and still not appear too anxious to see her.

Alicia saw him coming up the sidewalk when she opened the front door to get the morning paper. She had to agree with Chrissy's opinion that he looked like hell. But to her he was beautiful, and she wanted to wrap her arms around him. Instead she said a cool, "Hello, Pierce. Thank you for sending David the cards."

"How is his eye?"

"The stitches came out yesterday. It's amazing what a week can do. The scar's just a faint pink line. I told him that, in a year or two, that scar will drive the girls crazy."

He grinned. "What did David have to say about that?"

"Yuk. And that's a quote." He laughed and she shushed him. "They're still asleep."

"Our offspring seem intent on bringing us together," he remarked softly. "First David's accident, now this incident with Chrissy."

"Yes, it seems that way."

Then one of those silences descended and their eyes latched and held. Gluttonously they feasted on the sight of each other. He took in her wan complexion and she noted the dark bruises of fatigue ringing his eyes. He watched her breath shudder up through her chest, making her breasts tremble. He wanted to touch them, feel their lushness against his fingertips. She watched his pulse tick in the triangle at the base of his throat.

She wanted to press her lips there, feel his heartbeats against her lips.

Her eyelashes fluttered down to screen desire-clouded eyes. "Why don't you go in and talk to Chrissy while it's still peaceful? She's waiting for you. I'll bring in some coffee."

He reached for her hand and slowly drew her close to him. "Thanks for being her friend last night." He cupped her head, tilted it back, and kissed her softly on the mouth. Their eyes drifted open when they reluctantly backed apart. "Is she in the guest room?"

Alicia nodded dumbly and he went down the hall. Her heart was racing and her blood had heated with the merest touch of his lips. Damn! she cursed silently as she prepared a tray of coffee and cups. She had sworn to play it so aloof and here she was, quaking and quivering in front of him like a virgin before a god of fertility. One look from those green eyes, from beneath those sexy eyebrows, and her breasts had filled, the nipples swelling and tingling. Between her thighs . . . oh Lord.

So, he cared about the health of her son. So, he was a father, worried and vulnerable where his daughter was concerned. So, he was the best damn kisser in the whole damn universe. Was that any reason to come all undone? *Show some spunk, for heaven's sake. Some backbone. Don't let him get to you.*

Resolved not to be made a fool of again, she tapped on the door and Chrissy called for her to come in. They were sitting on the bed, which Chrissy had already made up. They were holding hands and Pierce was smiling. "Coffee?" Alicia asked and they both smiled a yes. She poured them each a cup, then made to leave.

"No, stay," Chrissy said, stretching out a hand and pulling Alicia down on the bed with them. "I'm just getting to the good part," she said with an impish grin. "When my future mother-in-law realized that I was serious, she said, 'Wherever will I wear that gown I bought for the wedding? It's quite unsuited to any other occasion.' "

They all three laughed, but Pierce heard Chrissy's sigh and touched her cheek. "No regrets, I hope."

Her matching eyes met his. "Only that I didn't see what I was letting myself in for sooner. How could I have been so stupid?"

"But you realized your mistake and did something about it. I'm very proud of the courage it took to do what you did."

"Daddy." Chrissy leaned forward and hugged him tight. They embraced warmly, unselfconsciously. Gone was the awkwardness between them. Alicia's throat knotted with emotion.

Before the scene became too maudlin, the door burst open and David and Adam came piling through it.

"Pierce, Chrissy!" they yelled in unison and hurled themselves onto the bed.

"Is this the day we're going to Disneyland?" David shrieked.

"Careful of the eye," Alicia called out warningly.

What ensued was an exchange of greetings and news that rivaled the noisy exchanges in the lobby of the United Nations. Everyone talked at once. Finally Adam shouted, "I want my breakfast."

"So what will you do now?" Pierce asked his daughter after the pancakes had been served. They were crowded around the table, but no one seemed to mind the bumping elbows.

"Today? Start looking for an apartment."

"You have an apartment," Pierce said, puzzled.

Chrissy was shaking her head. "That's Mother's

apartment. She found it, furnished it, she pays the bills."

"*I* pay the bills," Pierce said.

"Oops, sorry," she said. "Anyway I want a place of my own choosing. I want to start supporting myself. It'll be tough with classes and all, but I really want to do it, Daddy."

He winked his approval. Alicia was thinking. "Chrissy, could you do some sketches? Large, splashy, high-fashion ones?"

Chrissy laid her fork aside. "What did you have in mind?"

"To frame some sketches for the walls of the shops."

Chrissy's eyes widened. "You mean it, Alicia?"

"Yes. I've been thinking that the stores needed a face lift. I can see bright prints in brass frames. Very dramatic, very stylized, like the old covers of *Vogue*. They might just as well be your drawings."

"You wouldn't buy them simply because they were mine. I mean, if they weren't any good—"

"Make them good," Alicia challenged with a sly smile.

"Deal." Chrissy thrust her hand across the table and they shook hands hard.

She left a while later, wearing a pair of jeans and a sweater borrowed from Alicia. "I'll stay in touch."

"Do that," Alicia and Pierce called out at the same time as they waved to her from the front door. Her tread was jaunty and confident as she stepped into the Porsche.

"Can we go, Pierce? Can we?"

Alicia turned around to see David and Adam fairly dancing with excitement. "What is this about Disneyland?"

Abashedly, Pierce scratched his temple. "I promised David a trip to Disneyland if he was brave while Dr. Benedict sewed up his eye."

"I was brave."

"He was brave," Adam, who hadn't even been there, testified.

"Your mother and I will talk about it while we clean up the kitchen. Straighten your rooms, get dressed, brush your teeth, then we'll see."

"Yea! 'We'll see' usually means yes, Adam."

"Yea!"

Off they ran. Pierce took Alicia's hand and dragged her toward the kitchen. As soon as the door closed behind them, he pulled her against him and sought her lips with his.

She angled her head away. "I thought we were supposed to be doing the dishes."

"To hell with the dishes. I can't wait another minute to get my hands on you." He fastened her mouth to his.

She was still angry with him. Why was she letting him do this? Why was she standing here like warm putty waiting to be molded by his caresses? Beneath the mastery of his mouth, all her resolutions and hostility and avowals of avoidance vanished. She couldn't resist.

Not when his tongue was working its magic inside her mouth, pumping erotically, swirling lazily, igniting sparks of desire in every forbidden place of her body. Not when his hand was sliding beneath her top and covering her bare breast with a warm massaging palm. Not when his fingers were lightly plucking her nipple into a bead of passion.

The rational Alicia argued with the emotional one. She was doing it again, blindly plunging headlong toward more heartache. Masochistically, she was asking for rejection again. But at the moment she didn't care. How could she say no to him when everything inside her was crying out yes, yes, yes?

Pierce's brain was screaming admonitions to him, too, but his body had long since stopped listening to his brain. He had denied himself for as long as he could.

Damn the future and the risks. He'd take them. He wanted to give her the love that had filled his heart to bursting. Somehow he must convey to her that he knew now that his spirit was incomplete without her. Surely she knew how much his body required hers. The evidence pressed hard and throbbing between them.

"Don't do this to me again," she moaned into his mouth. Even as she spoke the denial, her hands locked around his neck and her tongue darted friskily past his lips.

"I'm sorry for every time I've hurt you." The heels of his hands coasted down the sides of her breasts. "I never wanted to hurt or disappoint you, Alicia. I swear that." His lips were ardent on her neck and the words he whispered across her flesh were erotic and scandalous and she loved every one of them.

He raised her top and dipped his knees to bring his head even with her breast. It filled his hand. The crest was flushed and tight with need. He rolled his tongue over it again and again until she was delirious. "Pierce, Pierce." His name slid through her lips sibilantly. He closed his mouth around her nipple and tugged with a sweet, rhythmic heat.

"God, this is insane." He came back to her mouth and regretfully lowered her top over a breast wet and shiny from his kiss. "Come here," he said roughly and hauled her down onto his lap as he sat in a chair. He burrowed his head between her breasts and nuzzled them. "If we don't stop I'm going to rape you on top of the breakfast table."

She bent her head over his, holding him tight to her, draping him with her hair. "I might not object to that."

"Ah, God, please, Alicia, don't move your bottom. You're killing me." But his hands went to her hips and held her securely over his lap. "How can anything that feels so damn good be such torture?"

Her lips found his ear and nibbled. "I sat on your lap that night at the cabin. You didn't seem to mind then." Her voice was a seductive drawl that emphasized the playfulness of her tongue.

"Then I wasn't zipped into a pair of jeans." He groaned as she lightly ground herself against him. "All right," he growled threateningly and her pulse nearly leaped out of her veins. "Two can play this game." Once again his hand slipped under her top. "I was kissing your breasts then, remember?"

"Uh-huh." Her eyes closed and her breath started coming fast and uneven.

"I was touching you with my tongue here." His fingertip slid down the outer curve of her breast. "Here." He outlined the deep bottom curve. "Here." He touched her nipple and she jumped in violent reaction. "Like this." He fanned her nipple with his fingertip and she cried out with remembrance and renewed longing. She collapsed against his chest.

He brought his hands from beneath her top and sank all ten fingers into the wealth of her hair. He pressed his forehead against hers. "Now is not the time nor the place, my love, or believe me, I'd already be deep inside you."

"Pierce!" She sighed, lifting her mouth from his kiss. "Will there ever be a time and place?"

He enfolded her in the tightest embrace. "God, I hope so. I hope so."

His lips opened over hers. He sealed their mouths solidly in a loving covenant. Her arms linked behind his head and she responded to the fervency of his kiss.

David and Adam bolted through the door. They all but skidded to a stop. Alicia and Pierce sprang apart.

"Mom and Pierce are having sex," David sang out to a tune of his own making. "Mom and Pierce are having sex."

Shocked by their sudden appearance and what her elder son was sing-songing, Alicia sat motionless on Pierce's lap, her arms still looped around his neck.

"David Russell, where did you hear that?"

"I made it up."

"Well, stop saying it. You don't even know what it means."

"I do so."

"What then?" she asked daringly, confident that he was boasting.

"It means hugging and kissing and lying down in bed together."

Her mouth fell open and she stared at him with rapidly blinking eyes. She turned toward Pierce in mute disbelief. He was grinning, one eyebrow cocked humorously. He shrugged. "You asked."

"See, I told you I know what sex means," David said, grinning proudly.

"I know too," Adam claimed.

Alicia stared at her children as though she'd never seen them before. Pierce was trying his best to suppress laughter but his shoulders were shaking. As solemnly as he could, he addressed David. "You may know all about it, but it's not something gentlemen discuss while ladies are around." Pierce nudged her and asked out the side of his mouth, "Did that sound too prudish?"

"Don't ask for my opinion. I didn't even know he knew the word."

"Why haven't you had a man-to-man talk with your sons before now?"

"I'm not a man."

His eyes slid down her front. "I noticed that," he said and the words slurred.

"Well, can we go? Why aren't the dishes done? We're ready."

"The dishes aren't done because Pierce and I were . . .

talking about Disneyland," Alicia said primly. She hopped off his lap and straightened her top and ran her fingers through her hair.

"You were not talking, you were kissing," Adam stated flatly.

"Well, yes, we were. . . a little," she admitted red-faced.

"Can we go?" David had a one-track mind.

Alicia glanced inquiringly at Pierce. "Yes, we can go!" he said. Over their squeals he shouted, "Go get jackets and caps, whatever you want to bring while we do the dishes."

David dashed out, but collided with Adam as he ran back in. "Are you going to do the dishes this time or are you going to start kissing again?"

"We're going to do the dishes," Pierce said, drawing an imaginary X across his heart. "I promise."

"Okay. Come on, Adam. Gee, can you believe it?"

Alicia and Pierce watched them go. They looked at each other and began to laugh. For long, wholesome, healthy minutes they laughed. "Do you really want to spend your Saturday off at Disneyland?" he asked, pulling her into his arms.

"Is that where you're going to be?" She laid her hands just inside his shirt collar and sifted her fingers through his chest hair.

"It looks like it."

"Then that's where I want to spend the day too." He ducked his head and kissed her. "You promised David you wouldn't start kissing me again," she murmured around his lips.

"I'm breaking my promise."

# *Eight*

The boys had the time of their lives. Pierce and Alicia were rarely without smiles. They strolled the Disney compound arm in arm or hand in hand, but somehow always touching. When they had to separate, their eyes remained in close contact. To anyone observing them, they were a couple in love.

Today belonged to them. Their conflict—to Alicia still a mystery—was shelved. They indulged their mutual fantasy. They pretended they were a family.

They ate and drank and laughed and clowned and finally coaxed a reluctant Adam to ride The Matterhorn.

"Don't be a baby," David scoffed. "It'll be great. Honest."

"Adam and I can sit this one out," Alicia offered.

"No!" Adam said, not wanting to lose face. "I want to ride it, only . . . Can I sit by Pierce?"

Pierce ruffled the boy's hair. "Sure thing. Who do you think I was counting on to hold my hand?"

Adam sat sandwiched between Pierce and Alicia. Eyes

shut and body tensed, he hunkered down between them. But he loved the ride and begged to ride it again. This time he rode in the front of the car, David behind him, then Alicia and Pierce. They straddled a padded seat.

"Pierce!" she said in a shocked whisper the moment their car entered the dark cavern. His hands went around her and wandered at will.

"Hmm?"

"I don't think that's allowed at Disneyland." No longer aware of the jerking, rocketing speed of the roller-coaster, her head dropped back onto his chest. The boys were screaming in delight, playing "spaceship," oblivious to the adults behind them.

Pierce's searching lips found her ear. "It's allowed if they don't catch you." His tongue feathered her earlobe. "Besides you've got no room to talk. Do you realize what you're doing to me?" He spread his hand wide over her stomach and drew her back even closer against him. She gasped when her bottom made contact with his crotch. He chuckled and kissed her neck and continued the heavy petting until the ride was over.

When they stepped back into the sunshine. Pierce's grin was that of the proverbial cat who got the cream. "As far as I'm concerned, we can't ride The Matterhorn often enough." Rosy color stained Alicia's cheeks and she quickly slipped her sunglasses on in hopes of hiding her blush.

"Come here, woman," Pierce growled caveman style and pulled her into his arms.

"Uh-oh," Adam said to his brother. "I think they're gonna start kissing again."

"No, we're not," Pierce said, laughing. "I'm just going to tell her a secret." Lifting her hair, he whispered something in her ear. Alicia pulled back and looked up at him in surprise. "How does that sound?" he asked.

"W-wonderful," she stammered. "But are you sure? Will you be too tired?"

"Will you?" She shook her head, smiling broadly. "Then go make your phone call. We'll be waiting in line at Dumbo."

When she joined them five minutes later she told Pierce, "All set."

"Terrific." He hugged her.

"What's all set?" David asked.

"Would you like to spend the night with Nana and Grandpa?"

"Do I look all right?" Alicia asked nervously as she gazed at herself in the mirror.

"Sure, you look fine," David said, not even lifting his head from the book he was flipping through. Adam yawned. His Mickey Mouse ears were sitting catty-cornered. He was so tired he didn't notice.

"Thanks a bunch," Alicia muttered. What had she expected? To them, she looked only like Mom. She wanted them to tell her she looked beautiful, ravishing, stunning. That's how she wanted Pierce to see her on this, their first actual date. She couldn't believe it when he had whispered the invitation in her ear while they were surrounded by the racket of Disneyland.

"Would your parents mind having the boys pawned off on them for one night? I'd like to take you to dinner, dancing, anything you want. Then I'd like to show you my house." That she was invited to spend the night had been implied. It had been hours ago, but her heart hadn't calmed down yet. She shouldn't go. *You can be hurt, Alicia*, she warned herself. But she wanted this night alone with him. What about tomorrow night? And the one after that?

"Why are you dressing up so much?" David interrupted her thoughts.

"I want to look nice for Pierce. He's taking me to dinner."

"Why can't we go?"

"It's a grown-up restaurant."

The doorbell rang. "I'll get it," the boys shouted in unison and raced from her bedroom. Adam was suddenly wide awake again.

Alicia was grateful for the few moments alone. She needed them to collect her wits. Did she look sophisticated, as if she went out with an attractive, successful man every weekend, as if it were nothing unusual? No. She looked flustered. She *was* flustered. Her hands were shaking as she misted herself with her most precious perfume.

What had happened to the campus beauty queen who had had young men vying for dates? She had fallen in love, married, born two children, lost her love. Firsthand knowledge of life's risks left one feeling less self-confident.

Somehow she had managed to bathe, shampoo and style her hair, and do her nails in a miraculously short time. She had chosen to wear a slinky black dress that clung to the curves of her body. The neckline draped and dipped low over her breasts, the hem swirled softly around her knees. She had on a smoky shade of stockings and high-heeled black shoes with rhinestone clips on the toes. Her hair was swept up into a loose knot and she'd purposefully disregarded the wispy tendrils that escaped it. Diamond studs adorned her ears and served as her only jewelry.

Assessing herself in the mirror, the verdict was that the lady-of-the-world image belied the trembling woman on the inside.

Taking up her purse and the overnight bag she had

discreetly packed for herself, she switched out the light and left the safety of her bedroom. For a moment she stood in the living room door watching as Pierce read to the boys from the Peter Pan picture book, David's souvenir from Disneyland. He had a boy under each arm snuggled close to him.

When he glanced up and saw her, he did a double take. Captain Hook could remain forever imperiled by the crocodile for all Pierce cared. The words of the story froze in his throat. The boys lifted their heads and, somehow sensing the intense emotion of the moment, remained blessedly quiet. Slowly Pierce disengaged himself and stood up. He came to her like someone induced by a hypnotist to walk. Indeed he was entranced.

"You look fabulous." He took her hands in his and dropped a reverent kiss on her cheek.

"Thank you." Her voice was silky, tremulous, infinitely but accidentally sexy.

"Ready?"

She nodded. They gathered up everything the boys were taking for their overnight stay at their grandparents' house. It wasn't easy, but they all managed to squeeze into Pierce's car. Her sons' enthusiasm over the car and their accumulated hyperactivity after a day at Disneyland combined to make Alicia tremendously glad to see her parents' house come into view.

Once the boys were handed over, good-byes were said, and Pierce and Alicia were alone in his car, he asked, "What did you tell your mother?"

"About what?"

"About why you wanted the boys to spend the night."

She twisted the small gold chain on her beaded handbag. "I said it would be simpler than getting them up in the middle of the night to take them home. I told her we planned to be out late."

"Do we?"

"Don't we?" Had she read him wrong? Was it only wishful thinking on her part that they would spend the night together? God! Did she look like an overanxious widow trying to trap a husband?

He reached across the console and took her hand, bringing it to his mouth. He raked his lips across her knuckles. "This isn't an audition, Alicia. We're playing it by ear. Why are you nervous?"

She laughed with shallow breathlessness. "I know it's ridiculous."

"Not ridiculous. Endearing," he said roughly.

"I just don't want you to think that I assumed—"

"I don't think anything except that you're the most desirable woman I've ever known. And I'm not only speaking in terms of sexuality. In every way, I find you fascinating. I need you in every way a man can need a woman. Your sweetness, your laughter, your caring." He turned her hand over and tickled her palm with his tongue. Sensations fluttered up from her thighs, through her womanhood, through every vital organ, to her breasts. "I'd love to share my bed with you tonight. But if not, it won't alter how I feel about you. I love you."

He braked the car in the driveway of the restaurant and, propping his arm on the back of the seat, turned to her. She stared at him speechlessly. He stroked the back of her hand with his thumb while his eyes ravished her face. "Alicia, no matter what happens, no matter . . ."

He stopped, looked down at their clasped hands, then began again. "I want you to know that today was one of the finest, most productive days of my life. I love your boys. I love you. With all my heart. Nothing, *nothing* can or will ever change that."

Leaning across the console, he laid his lips on hers and kissed her. With only their hands and lips touching, he drew her to him as inexorably as if he had wound velvet cords around her and reeled her in. She laid her free hand on his lapel and tilted her head for a more cohesive contact with his mouth. She felt that all she was was flowing into him, melding with him. Her lips parted as his tongue slid sinuously between them to touch the tip of hers.

The door on the driver's side was suddenly opened. "Ooops, sorry, Mr. Reynolds."

"It's okay," Pierce said to the valet. He withdrew from her but kept his eyes on her face. "We're ready to go in now."

Alicia wasn't sure she was. At that moment she didn't know if she could walk, stand, breathe. Her reflexes were chasing recklessly through her body, her mind was spinning, her soul was soaring. She had been completely disoriented by Pierce's spellbinding embrace and had willingly given herself over to its obsessive power. She had wanted to be held its bewitched victim forever.

His kiss, like a magic vapor, had wafted through her body, stroking the back of her throat, her breasts, her stomach, the cleft between her thighs, the backs of her knees, the soles of her feet.

Still dazed, she was handed out of the car. Adroitly, Pierce ushered her through the glass doors of the restaurant, outrageously tipping the valet who had disturbed their kiss.

The restaurant wasn't one of the glitzy places where celebrities and would-be celebrities came to flash newly installed Hollywood caps, try out new face lifts, and spot Rodeo Drive chic. It was refined, understated, elegant. The decor was as subdued as the music being played by the violin and piano duo. The army of waiters was deferential and all but invisible and silent.

"Your table is ready, Mr. Reynolds," the *maître d'* murmured as he greeted them. "This way."

As they followed him, heads turned in their direction. Without conceit Alicia had to admit they made a striking couple. Pierce's suit was dark charcoal, almost black. His shirt was ivory and the silk tie and the handkerchief he had arranged in his breast pocket were the color of vintage burgundy wine. His hair gleamed and looked well-groomed, but still retained that roguish dishevelment, as though a whimsical breeze, or a woman's fingers, had lightly tossed through it.

When they were seated and Pierce was looking over the wine list, Alicia remarked coolly, "Everyone seems to know you. Do you come here often?"

He grinned at her less-than-subtle display of jealousy. "I entertain potential clients here frequently."

"They should be impressed."

"They are. After a dinner meeting here, we're usually guaranteed the job." He mischievously didn't satisfy her female curiosity about any woman companions he might have brought to the restaurant. They were irrelevant anyway. "What are we going to eat? Do we want red or white wine?"

She couldn't have said later what she ate. All she knew was that it was delicious. Her taste buds were awakened to delightful textures and varied flavors. But all her senses were heightened. She was high and it had nothing to do with the wine.

"My stomach won't know what to think." The waiter was taking away her entree plate. "It's used to hamburger and fast foods."

"I'm glad you enjoyed it. I recommend the strawberries Romanoff for dessert."

"I couldn't, really."

She could, she did, she loved every sinful morsel.

"Pierce?"

"Hmm?" He took her hand across the candlelit table and their waiter, knowing they wouldn't need him anymore, intuitively glided away.

"Forgive me if I'm prying," she began. "You often put

down your professional success, make light of it. Why? Most men would flaunt it."

He turned her hand palm up and tracked the faint lines with his fingertip. "I don't feel successful, Alicia. Recently I woke up to the fact that everything in my life could be measured by a financial chart. Is that success? Once I thought so. Not anymore."

"You seem to have your priorities straight. However, financial and professional success aren't anything to be ashamed of."

"When they're all your life truly counts for, maybe they are."

"I don't understand you," she said, shaking her head. "Why are you so self-critical?"

"Where are the wife, the children, the home a man my age should have? After my failed first marriage, I never saw fit to commit myself to another, mostly because of indifference and downright laziness. Only in the last couple of weeks have I been any kind of parent to my daughter. God, I regret all those years Chrissy and I could have meant something to each other and didn't. And it sure as hell wasn't her fault. In the areas of life that really should count for something, I feel like a bum. I have nothing to be proud of." He cradled her cheek in his palm and she leaned her face into it. "That's why I wish . . ."

"Wish what?"

His eyes fell away and the seconds ponderously ticked by. At last he looked at her again, and his introspective expression had changed. She knew he had closed the subject. "I wish you'd go dancing with me tonight. Do you like to dance?"

They went to one of the posh new clubs where virtually any shape, form, and age of human being could be spotted. From punks with pink and blue hair to ladies swathed in chinchilla, all types were represented. The mirrored floor reflected the madly gyrating bodies. Motion pictures, everything from Charlie Chaplin to erotica, flickered on the walls. The music blared, an insult to any discerning eardrum.

"Are you the same man who bought a Donald Duck T-shirt this afternoon?" Alicia had to scream to her partner over the pounding bass and shrill treble.

"The same. And are you the lady who likes ice cream cones and merry-go-rounds?"

"I confess." She twirled, showing a good portion of thigh. "But this is fun too."

"The only problem is—"

"What?" she shouted, holding a hand to her ear.

He came closer and put his hands on her waist. "I said the only problem is that they never play any slow dances. The guys never get to hold the girls."

"That's because too often they can't tell one from the other."

"That's true," he said, laughing. "But I sure can tell you're a girl." His hands slid up her sides, the heels of them brushing her breasts and applying a slight, but unmistakable, pressure. There was also no mistaking the gleaming heat in his eyes. "I know a place where we can slow dance."

Alicia didn't protest when he took her hand and guided her through the raucous crowd. He drove with his right hand on her knee when it wasn't shifting the gears of the sports car. His house was in the hills overlooking the city and Alicia, whose family had always been affluent, was awed when he drew up to iron gates and opened them with a transmitter. The lawn was landscaped and immaculate, the driveway wide. He pulled the car to a stop in front of a sprawling ranch-style house.

"Don't be too impressed," he said derisively. "It's only a big, empty house."

"A beautiful house."

"That's why it's such a pity that it's empty. Someone should be enjoying it. No one ever has."

The interior of the house was everything the exterior promised. The rooms were spacious and well laid out, tastefully and expensively decorated in California casual. Area rugs dotted shining hardwood floors. The ceilings were high and beamed. Immodestly undraped windows offered breathtaking vistas of the city lights spread out in a twinkling blanket below.

"It's beautiful, Pierce."

"It is now." He pulled her close and hugged her hard, slowly swaying back and forth. "You do wonders for this house and it feels so right having you here."

His lips were warm as they moved over hers. Lightly, briefly, tantalizingly. They slid to her neck, across her jaw, behind her ear, down her throat. "Would you like something to drink?"

"Would you have to stop doing this to fix it?"

"Yes."

"No, thank you."

His smile melted against hers and his tongue imbedded itself in the warm, wet silkiness of her mouth. His hands massaged their way down her back, past her waist. He cupped her derrière and boldly urged her against his hard heat. She adjusted herself to it and felt the rumble of approval and arousal in his chest. Her arms, feeling weighted down with a delicious lassitude, but oddly defying gravity, lifted languorously around his neck. Her fingernails teased the lobes of his ears.

"I thought we came here to slow dance." His expression was teasing as he raised his head. His nose batted playfully against hers.

"By all means. I was only biding my time until you asked me. Where's the music?"

He coiled an arm around her waist and guided her to a

wall of bookshelves where the components of a stereo system were arranged. The control panel looked more intricate than that of an airplane, but with a flip of several switches, soft music began to emanate from strategically placed speakers.

Alicia floated into his embrace once again. His arms folded behind her back at her waist. She crossed hers behind his neck and laid her head on his chest.

His lips moved in her hair. "Do you know what I first noticed about you?"

"My stupidity. You couldn't believe anybody would go to the woods for a week without a lantern."

He laughed. "Before that."

"So you *did* think I was stupid."

"Maybe just a little scatterbrained."

"Well it couldn't have been my looks that captured your attention because as I recall I looked like a drowned rat. It must have been my sparkling conversation."

"You were stuttering."

"How chivalrous of you to remind me."

"Give up? It was this." He caressed her fanny, sliding his hands over the gentle swelling.

She pushed away from him, feigning indignation. "Of all the base, rude, prurient, chauvinistic, sexist—"

"It was all I could see," he claimed self-defensively, and brought her back to him swiftly with a soft thud of her breasts against his chest. "It's about the cutest fanny I've ever seen."

"And you've evaluated many, I suppose?"

"Jealous?"

"Pea green with it."

"Good."

She was rank with jealousy, jealous of every woman who had ever been held in his arms, caressed by his hands, kissed by his mouth. How many had he brought to this house on the pretext of a slow dance? How many had been moved through the rooms in what, not by any stretch of the imagination, could be called a waltz?

"You've got no reason to be jealous of anyone." His whispering lips found hers again. It was a kiss that drew all the life out of her, drained her, yet made her feel more alive than she ever had.

When at last he freed her mouth from the sweet suction of his, her eyes opened reluctantly. She hadn't noticed when they'd left one room and entered another. It had all been one sensuous journey through time, through space. Now she noted that they were in a game room and her bottom was being pressed against a billiard table. "Do you, uh, play?" Her voice was mere puffs of air that somehow fashioned themselves into words.

"Uh-huh." Delightfully imprisoning her against the table by pressing his middle into hers, he began to remove the pins from her hair. Each one was sought after by nimble fingers, pinched between them, and extracted with utmost care, slowly, as though he were peeling away a garment. Her hair cascaded over his hands like spilled molten gold. He nestled his face in it.

"Is it hard to do?"

"Uh-huh."

"Are you very good?"

"Expert."

His hands were on her breasts now, rubbing softly, and she moaned. "You must have developed a winning technique."

"It's all in the way you line up your balls and aim your cue."

She dragged her mouth from beneath the drugging power of his and looked at him through eyes narrowed with suspicion. "Are we still talking about pool?"

His eyebrows jumped mischievously. "Of course. What did you think?" His hands spanned her waist and easily lifted her onto the table. It took no more than a gentle pressure of his hands on her shoulders for her to lie back. He followed her down onto the green felt, covering her body with his. Insistent lips claimed hers. His tongue swept her mouth like a torch and set off a wild-fire that uncontrollably spread through her body.

With his fingers buried in her hair, he rolled them over until she was on top. She kissed back fiercely, seduced by the hedonistic promise of his mouth. Making increasingly urgent sounds in his throat, he lowered the zipper of her dress with measured care and then brought his hand around to her front. Hooking his index finger in the cloth, he lowered the loosened bodice. The tops of her breasts swelled over the lacy border of her brassiere. He caressed her with his eyes, then with his fingertips, then with his mouth. He raised his head off the table, his passion mounting with each kiss.

"Pierce," she sighed. She moved against him sinuously, like a cosseted pet against its owner. "This is decadent."

"Purely decadent." His chin scoured her gently. He nipped her lightly with his teeth. "You're delicious."

"I'm the mother of two children," she groaned softly. His tongue was lashing her thrillingly.

"And you have the sumptuous breasts to prove it. Oh God, Alicia, I need you."

He turned them again and stared down at her with the question burning in his eyes. Her hair was fanned out behind her head on the green felt, lending her an air of defenselessness. Her eyes were limpid with desire and her lips were soft and moist and inviting. She lay with her arms flung to her sides, vulnerable and wanton. She looked both an innocent and a temptress. Pierce wanted them both.

Without a word he helped her off the table and led her down the hall into the bedroom he had showed her earlier. He offered no apology for the romantic ambiance he had purposefully created. The lights were dimmed. Music was piped in from some unknown source. In a silver wine bucket, a bottle of champagne was chilling.

On their way through the living room, he had picked up the overnight bag she had left there earlier. He handed it to her now and smiled tenderly. "Don't feel like you owe me anything. I'll take you home now if you want."

She had never loved him more than she did at that moment. He was thinking of her, not of himself. She touched his mouth with her fingertip. "I'm staying. And, Pierce," she said, lowering her voice and looking away timidly. "I saw my gynecologist and took care of . . . you know." She didn't meet his eyes before she moved away.

In his opulent bathroom she found something that surprised and touched her with its blatant sentimentality. It bespoke a request that Pierce would never verbalize. She smiled tenderly as she began to undress.

Before she opened the door she switched off the light, so she stepped into shadows. He was sitting on the side of the bed opening the champagne. He lifted his eyes to her and they gleamed hot and green from across the room. "Let me see you."

As she moved, the black negligee floated around her as sheer and soft and alluring as a fallen angel's wings. "When did you get this?"

He stood up. He was wearing a short wrapper like a karate pajama. It came to mid-thigh. It was grey and piped in green. He looked wonderful in it, his chest wide and hair-dusted in the deep V opening that came to a point at his waist. His legs were lean and well formed, muscled from his jogging regimen.

"I stole it from the cabin when I left." His shy confession made her heart ache with love. "I didn't plan ever to see you in it. I just wanted to keep it." When he came to her, he encircled her neck with his fingers. "I've imagined you wearing it a thousand times, but you far surpass any fantasy."

Her body was clearly defined beneath the transparent fabric. His eyes adored every nuance. It took unbearable discipline, but he contented himself with kissing her softly, brushing his lips over hers. In his mind, this was their wedding night. He was going to treat her like his bride, cherish her. "Drink some champagne with me."

He poured only one glass and offered it to her first. She drank. The bubbly wine was deliciously cold and biting on her tongue, but not nearly as intoxicating as Pierce. She imbibed his scent, the color of his skin and hair and eyes, the textures of his body, the planes and angles of his face.

While she still held the glass, he lifted it to his lips and drank, tasting more of her than the champagne. Then setting the glass aside, he drew her down on the bed. While she watched in avid fascination, he loosened the knot at his waist and shrugged out of the wrapper.

His virile nakedness excited her and made her insides curl warmly and gravitate toward her pulsing center. She wanted to lasciviously gobble up every inch of him with her eyes. How could she, Alicia Russell, be so brazenly lustful of the naked male body? But it wasn't just that alone. It was Pierce. And she loved him. As splendid as the body was, it was the whole man she reached out for.

He knelt beside her. Starting with her face, he surveyed her lovingly. His eyes were poetic in their appreciation. "I love your mouth." He outlined it with his finger. "The way it's shaped, the way it feels." She dared to touch his fingertip with her tongue. His gasp was quick and sharp. Emboldened, she closed her lips around him and sucked lightly. "My God, Alicia," he murmured. He lowered his head and, removing his finger from between her lips, replaced it with his tongue.

They almost got carried away. He forced himself to lift his head from her kiss. His hands combed down her chest and smoothed over her breasts. Her nipples pressed against the gossamer confines of the nightgown. Bending over her, he licked one, his tongue scratching over the lace.

"Oh, Pierce, Pierce." She tossed her head on the pillows and caught handfuls of his hair in restless fingers. His caresses were bold and proficient and soon she was writhing beneath his fervor.

Her response made him a little wild. He kissed her stomach randomly, examined her navel with an inquisitive tongue, caressed lower until she felt his touch on the mound of her femininity. Gently he nudged her thighs apart and lay between them. He raised the gown. She felt the moist caresses of his mouth on the skin of her abdomen, in the soft triangle of down, on her thighs. Between them.

Deftly he caressed with suppliant lips and agile tongue. She approached that divine death again and again, only to be brought back, detained, postponed by bliss. No longer able to breathe, she cried out for fulfillment. He obliged. He touched the source of all her desire and lifted the floodgate of her passion.

Her heart exploded in a blinding light. Her body quickened and surged against him. She knew the most intense rush of pleasure she'd ever known and sobbed when the ecstasy of it tore through her chest and belly. When she finally coasted down from the pinnacle, she was appalled at herself and turned her head away when he raised himself above her. Her cheeks were stained with tears.

"You're so beautiful to me. All of you. Please don't cry." The words stirred against her mouth. With a finger under her chin, he forced her to look at him. "I would never do anything to offend you. I love you, Alicia. I only wanted to demonstrate how much."

She flung her arms around him. "Oh, my darling, it's nothing you did that's making me cry." Tears were leaking from the corners of her eyes, but they were joyous tears. "I just can't believe that anyone could love so unselfishly, could love *me* so much."

They kissed. Her hand scaled down his body in an orgy of feeling, cataloguing each discovery. His chest was wide, furred, sculpted. His stomach was flat and taut. The hair tapered down to a silky ribbon that her fingertips tracked. She ventured farther and his breathing began to rasp loudly in her ear. When her fingers closed around him, he buried his head between her breasts and moaned her name. Wanting to give back a portion of his gift to her, she caressed until he could bear no more.

They came together in one swift, plunging fusion. He held her tight, not moving, only savoring the unspeakable rapture of being gloved by her body. Then slowly he began to stroke her.

"Never forget that I love you," he whispered urgently. "I love you, Alicia. Remember that always. I love you."

"And I you." She wrapped herself around him, bringing him as deeply into her as possible. "I love you so much."

"Darling, my love." He held back until she shuddered beneath him again, her body milking his. Then he surrendered his soul and let his body bathe her with his love.

". . . and Nana made pizza for our supper except it wasn't the frozen kind like you cook. She made it out of a bowl."

"Thanks, Nana," Alicia said dryly, and Pierce smiled. From the time they had picked them up, the boys had talked nonstop, reporting everything that had transpired since they had left them.

"Grandpa played checkers with us, but I think he let us win."

"We ate popcorn while we watched television. And Nana made waffles and sausage for breakfast." Adam's good times were measured by his stomach. "She gave us candy because we ate all our breakfast."

Alicia rolled her eyes heavenward. "Next week we'll be going to the dentist. A day at Disneyland and overnight with Nana is like taking an injection of sugar into every tooth."

"We had a great time," David said. "Did you have fun too?"

Pierce slid a meaningful glance in Alicia's direction and she blushed, something she thought she would never do again after the night they had shared. "Yes, we had a terrific time," he drawled.

"What did you do?"

"Oh, lots of fun things," was Pierce's blithe reply and Alicia's cheeks went a brighter pink. He laughed out loud.

At the door of the house she told the boys to take their overnight bags into their rooms and unpack them. "Put everything back where it belongs, please."

Just before entering the hall, David turned back. "I almost forgot. I wanted to ask Pierce something."

By tacit agreement, Alicia and Pierce weren't keeping their affection a secret from the boys. He had his arm around her shoulders and her arms were loosely around his waist. Her head was resting comfortably on his chest.

"What's that?" Pierce asked.

"My Cub Scout pack is going on an overnight camp-out. Since I don't have a dad they said I could invite somebody else. I was gonna ask Carter. But I'd rather ask you."

"Thanks for the honor," Pierce said, smiling. He fingered Alicia's hair in an absently loving manner. "When is it?"

"Next month."

Alicia felt Pierce's withdrawal immediately. He seemed to shrink away from her, draw into himself, erect an invisible wall and close them off. His hand dropped from its caress of her hair, the arm around her shoulder tensed, then fell away to dangle lifelessly at his side. His whole body went stiff and resistant.

Her head came up; she pushed away to better see him. His face was blank, his eyes hollow. She knew he had retreated into that no man's land again. But this time rather than feeling despair, she felt anger. How dare he do this to her after yesterday, after last night, after all his avowals of love.

"Will you, Pierce?" David asked.

"We'll talk about it later, David," she said, forcing gentleness into her voice when she felt like screaming. "Go do as I asked. You and Adam rest in your rooms for a while, watch television. Pierce and I want to talk."

"Okay," he said dispiritedly and ambled off down the hall.

Pierce was staring at the floor. When David was out of earshot, he raised his head. His eyes were cold. "I won't be able to go with him. Please make my excuses."

"Like hell I will," she spat out. "Who is going to make your excuses to me? You're about to pull another disappearing act, aren't you?" She gripped him by the upper arms and shook him as hard as she could. She'd never been a fighter, a person who sought a physical outlet for her anger, but she was trembling with fury and wanted to strike him. "Well, this time I want to know why. How can you freeze up like this after last night?"

"Last night was the most beautiful night of my life. I meant it when I said I love you."

"Then why?" she shouted. "Why are you walking out again? And that's what you're about to do, isn't it?"

"Yes."

"And this time there will be no family intervention, will there? You won't be coming back, will you?"

His eyes bore into hers. His jaw was rigid. "No. I won't be coming back."

She recoiled. She hadn't thought he'd say it with such absolute conviction. He had called her bluff and now she was sorry she'd forced it. "After yesterday?" Her voice wasn't cooperating. It was breaking up with pain when she wanted it to reveal all the angry hate she felt for him at that moment. "After yesterday, you can just walk out without a backward glance?"

"I have to."

"Stop saying that. You don't!"

"I do."

"Why?"

"I can't afford to stay with you, with the boys, any longer. It will only make things harder if I do. Believe me it's best for everyone if we break it off now."

"I don't believe that."

"Believe it."

"Last night meant nothing to you?"

He rounded on her and grasped her shoulders. He brought her against him hard. The impact took her breath. His face was fierce, the words were strained through his teeth. "Last night meant everything to me. It was my deepest wish enacted. I could pretend that we were married, that we belonged to each other, that we had a future."

"Oh God, Pierce." She wanted to tear at her hair, to

claw at her skin in frustration. "How can you say all that when you plan to leave me? How?"

"Don't you know how difficult it is for me to walk away from you? Don't you know that your body, since the first time we made love in the cabin, is a part of mine? I'd as soon cut out my heart as leave you. It will be the same. You're a part of me, Alicia. Forever. The sweet personalities of your boys are a part of my soul now and always will be." He squeezed his eyes shut and enunciated each word precisely. "But I can't see you anymore."

She was crying. She damned the tears, but they collected in her eyes and rolled down her cheeks anyway. She damned herself for begging, but she had to. He couldn't leave her. She wouldn't let him. She caught handfuls of his shirt in her hands and lightly beat her fists on his chest. "Tell me why. *Why?*"

"Don't make it harder than it is."

"It couldn't be any harder."

"You don't want to know."

"I do."

"You don't."

"Tell me."

"No."

"Tell me, damn you!"

"I'm dying!"

# *Nine*

No, he wasn't dying. She was.

Life leaked out of her body by slow degrees. The tears were instantly checked as though his announcement had dried up everything inside her. She stood perfectly still, not so much as an eyelash moving.

It was he who moved. He gently pried her hands off his shirt front and backed away. He felt her pain as keenly as if someone had plunged a knife into his heart. It wracked the features of his face. Distorted them. He couldn't bear her suffering and turned away from it. He went to stand at the window. It was a clear, smog-free day. It didn't deserve to be.

Alicia stood there, petrified, for an interminably long time. Neither of them was counting the minutes. At last she drew in a staggering breath that seemed to puncture her lungs as though they were virgin. The blood finally, sluggishly, began to pump through her body again. Her veins seemed unwilling to accept it, filled to capacity as they were with misery. She wiped her cheeks with the backs of her hands. Her face was stiff from the salty tears drying on it.

She looked at him and the tears started again, but she didn't let them fall. He was so hard, so solid. She searched for, but couldn't find, one trace of frailty in him. She knew, didn't she, his strength, his endurance? My God! She could still feel his power bursting inside her.

"That's impossible."

He looked at her over his shoulder. "That's what I said when they told me. It's possible. Not for certain, but very possible."

She shook her head in miscomprehension. "Don't talk to me in half-truths and riddles. Please."

"Sit down," he commanded softly. "You look about ready to drop."

She stumbled her way to the sofa and folded down onto it like a collapsible paper doll hinged at the joints. "There's nothing wrong with you," she insisted.

"I couldn't believe there was either. I went in for my regular yearly checkup. It was an inconvenience, a nuisance, something that I had to juggle my schedule around in order to do. I certainly didn't worry about the outcome." He paced as he talked. "It's something in my blood. They told me it could be a condition treatable with proper medication or—" He stopped abruptly and looked at her. "A rare disease that is degenerative and terminal."

She covered her mouth with cold fingers to keep her lips from quivering. She wanted to weep, to let go and sob hysterically, to bang her head against the wall, to scream. But she knew she couldn't. "They don't know for sure?"

He shook his head. "They told me it would take about three weeks to get a firm diagnosis. They had to send blood samples back east somewhere for extensive and sophisticated testing. The symptoms of the conditions are so similar that it takes a while to establish which it is. Some of the cultures take days." Impatiently he flung his hands wide. "I don't want to talk about that." He raked back his hair. "I found out two days before I met you. That's why I had gone to the cabin. To think. To adjust to the fact that in a few months I might be dead."

A garbled cry escaped her lips before she could clamp a hand over it. Tears spurted from her eyes. He rushed forward and knelt in front of her. "Alicia, don't. This is why I never wanted you to know. You would have been better off thinking I was a sonofabitch who took what I wanted from you and then skipped."

She touched his hair. "You're not sick. You can't be sick."

He sprang up and began his pacing again. He was angry. "I argued that point too. It's damned unfair. I jog, I take vitamins. When I noticed the first sign of a paunch, I joined a health club, lost fifteen pounds, began working out religiously three times a week. I eat right. I don't drink too much. I stopped smoking years ago when the first breath of warnings against it were sounded. I think I could accept what they told me if I felt bad, if I were in pain, if I were weak, if I couldn't make love to you all night and feel ready to do it again with the slightest stimulation."

She looked away because the reminders were too vivid, the recollections too fresh. "When will you know?"

"In a few days I suppose. The three weeks are about up."

She raised her head hopefully. "Maybe—"

He was shaking his head adamantly even as he interrupted her. "No, Alicia. I have to plan for the worst. I couldn't base anything on hope because . . . Well, I couldn't. I couldn't stand the disappointment."

Her chest caved in on itself. She could feel everything

inside her sinking, shrinking, sagging. He sat down beside her and took her hand. "Do you see why I told you from the beginning that I couldn't get involved? I didn't want to hurt you. If you hadn't been you, if you'd been just another attractive woman, I'd have had you in bed that first night. I would have used you to relieve my mental anguish, I would have emptied all my despair into your body and wouldn't have cared if I never saw you again."

He released her hand and went to the window again. His voice was low, deep, rife and rusty with emotion. "But you *were* you. And I knew that if I had you once, I wouldn't want to let you go. You were exactly what I needed. But I knew I was the last thing you needed."

He faced her. "You are a young woman who has already lost one man. You have two sons who need a father. You need a man who can make a home for you, give you years of happiness and love."

He sat on a chair opposite her and pleaded for her forgiveness with his eyes. "I knew it was wrong of me to make love to you that night Chrissy came to the cabin, but I couldn't stop myself then. And I couldn't stop myself from coming back each time I did, knowing damn well that I shouldn't ever see you again. That night after David's accident, I knew you wanted me to stay. I wanted to. You needed comfort and love and the reassurance that you weren't all alone in the world. I couldn't give you that security. Even though I knew it insulted you, hurt your pride, made you angry, I forced myself to leave. You and the boys were like a gift handed to me, but you came too late."

He stood again, thumping his fists against his thighs. He looked like a man frustrated past his limit, who at any moment he might fly into a raging fit. "I've taken stock of my life. One starts doing that when he realizes his mortality. You and David and Adam were like a breath of fresh air. I wanted the chance you afforded to make something meaningful out of my life. I would have loved to be a husband to you, to make love to you every night, to share confidences and laughter and even heartaches. I would have loved for us to have a baby. I would have liked to be the father your boys need, to watch them grow up, help them when I could, encourage them from the sidelines when I couldn't. I want all that, Alicia. But it's too late. Too damn late." He returned to his position by the window.

They didn't speak for a long while. She wanted to comfort him, alleviate his suffering. But she couldn't. He wouldn't tolerate pity. And who would comfort her? Her heart had finally healed itself after Jim's death. With time it had knitted itself back together, repaired the break. Now, where her heart used to be, there was only a giant, gaping wound. This time she didn't think it would ever heal.

"What will you do?" she asked at last.

"You mean if—"

"Yes."

"Sell my part of the company to the other partners. Liquidate everything. Visit my mother. Then leave. Disappear. I couldn't bear a deathwatch."

She flinched against the word and shuddered as though the temperature in the room had dropped drastically. "Does Chrissy know?"

He shook his head. "No one. That's how I wanted it."

"That's cruel, Pierce. Your mother and Chrissy should be told. You've only just established a relationship with your daughter. She would want to know."

"Would you have wanted to know that Jim was going to die that day?"

Her mouth twisted with hurt as though he'd slapped her. Furious with himself, he cursed. "I'm sorry. I'm sorry," he repeated shaking his head. "This isn't how I wanted it to be. I wanted it to be a clean, quick break. Leaving you angry would have been so much better than this. I can't stand myself for forcing this sorrow on you." He took a deep breath. "I'm leaving now, Alicia."

He went to the door and she vaulted off the sofa, desperate not to let him out of her sight. "I'll never see you again?" she asked frantically.

He closed his eyes briefly and shook his head. "No," was his quiet answer.

"But—" She stopped herself. How could she be so selfish? She had been on the verge of telling him to call her if the worst proved false, if the blood tests wrote a happier ending to the story. *Call me if everything is all right, but don't bother if it's not.* That was the essence of what she was about to say.

He understood. He came to her and tenderly stroked her cheek with the backs of his knuckles, a bittersweet smile on his lips. "We've said everything that needs to be said. More. I ask nothing of you, Alicia. I knew from the beginning that anything between us would be impossible, but I couldn't help involving you." His eyes rained love over her face. "Forgive me. I loved you too much."

The door closed behind him. And still she stood in the middle of the room unable to move.

*"I've never done this before."*

*"Drunk champagne in a hot tub? It's a must for every orgy."*

*"What are you looking at?"*

*"Your breasts."*

*"That's what I thought."*

*"I love the way the water bubbles over your nipples."* He took champagne in his mouth, lifted her high against him and fastened his lips around her nipple. His mouth was cold against her hot skin.

"Oh, how can anything feel that good?" Wet hands gripped his wet hair.

He lifted her out of the tub and laid her on the redwood decking. Taking up the bottle of champagne, he tilted it and dribbled the sparkling wine over her. She shivered. But not from cold. From the tongue that followed the naughty rivulets of champagne.

"The candles were a good idea. I should have thought of them."

"I love candlelight."

"I love the way it looks on your skin." She could feel his eyes traveling the naked length of her back as she lay with her chin propped on his breastbone. Her thighs lay between his. "I like the way your hair spills across my chest. It's a very erotic picture."

"The candles smell good." She breathed deeply and the scent of flowers and spices filled her head.

"You smell good." Idly his fingers feathered up and down her sides, making her shiver.

"So do you."

"What do I smell like?"

She lifted her head and stared at him dreamily. "Like man. Like me. Like us. Together." His fingers sifted through her hair, massaged her scalp. "What do you taste like, Pierce?"

His hands stilled. He held his breath as she seductively inched down his body. Her fingers touched him. He groaned. Her lips. He died. And then he was reborn.

"I can't brush my hair while you're doing that." They were dressed and almost ready to leave. Her arms were raised to her hair as she stood at the bathroom dressing table. He was behind her, reaching around her to fondle her breasts.

"Why bother? I'll probably just mess it up again. Thank you for not wearing a bra today."

His thumbs were doing provocative things to her nipples. Slowly, softly, softly. Alicia watched his hands in the mirror, watched the response of her own body, saw the smoky hues of passion rising in her eyes, in his. She lowered her arms and dropped the brush with a clatter that went unheeded. Her bottom pressed snugly against the hard ridge beneath his fly. "We're already dressed," she complained breathlessly.

"Uh-huh." His grin was wicked. Clothes would be no deterrent to him at all. He turned her around, unzipped her slacks, unzipped his. He drew her close. Close. So close. Until they were one.


Alicia sat up in bed, sweat and tears pouring down her face.

All day she had coped. She had been a good mother, meeting the physical needs of her sons. She had fed them when she didn't think she'd ever be hungry again. She had listened to their chatter when she wanted to scream at them to be quiet and leave her in peace. She went through the ordeal of preparing them for bed and getting things ready for school the next day when she didn't want to move, but only wanted to curl up in a fetal ball. The last thing she felt like doing was smiling, but she had even forced smiles onto her lips when the boys expected them.

She had done all that and managed to perform an act of believable normalcy. On a day when her limbs felt like strapped-on weights that didn't want to budge, when her body knew a lethargy, an apathy for life that was frightening, she had survived by a sheer act of will.

But now, in her own bed, she could pamper her dejection. Her memories were thieves of sleep and unconsciousness. They wouldn't let her forget or ignore. They haunted her.

*Forgive me. I loved you too much.*

She rolled to her side and wept, wept bitterly and wetly, until she was drained of tears, of spirit, of hope.

For the next two days she lived in a vacuum, acting out her life. At work she was devoid of ideas and quick to criticize those offered by others. Everyone noticed the change from her usual effervescence. One cohort braved to ask if something were wrong. Alicia snapped back, saying that she was just tired.

She tried to keep her despair at bay around the boys. But, of course, they bore the brunt of her mood. She hated herself every time she showed them her temper when she didn't think she could stand their incessant chatter any longer. Unfortunately, like most children, they didn't take hints too well and often brought Pierce's name into the conversation.

"Is Pierce going on the camp-out with me?"

"I don't think so, David. You'd better ask Carter. Or maybe Grandpa. He'd like that."

"But I want Pierce."

"Well, he can't go."

"Why?"

"Eat your dinner."

"Why can't Pierce go? Why doesn't he come to see us? Did you make him mad again?"

"Eat your dinner!" She stood up, flung down her napkin, and ran from the room so they wouldn't see her tears. Later she spent a long time with them over a bedtime story, tucking them in and kissing them good night. They didn't mention Pierce again, but she could see the questions in their soulful eyes. Hopefully they would soon forget him.

Everyday activities seemed Herculean tasks. Lifting a milk carton out of the refrigerator, getting dressed for work in the morning, driving the car pool to soccer practice, all required more energy than she could garner. She felt like doing nothing but sitting motionless, talking to no one, staring into space, demanding of God what horrendous thing she had done to deserve punishment like this.

That's what she was doing on Wednesday morning when the telephone rang. The boys' ride to school had picked them up. Alicia hadn't finished dressing, but she was absently sipping a cup of coffee, dreading the rush hour traffic, the day, the rest of her life.

"Hello."

"How's my favorite girl? Ouch! Damn, Sloan, those nails are sharp. Boy, pregnant ladies can sure get mean." Kissing sounds. "Make that, how's my second favorite girl?"

In spite of her black mood, Alicia smiled into the phone. "Carter? Sloan?"

"You remember us? We were beginning to wonder. We haven't heard from you."

"I'm sorry." Listlessly she plucked at the telephone cord and watched it wobble. It was good to hear Carter's voice. A friend. Tears were blurring her eyes. "I've been busy. I took that job I told you about."

"That's terrific. She took the job." He was passing the news on to Sloan. "Ask her what? Hey, wait a minute. I can see how this is going to go. Why don't you take this extension and I'll go to the one in the office."

"Hi, Alicia," Sloan said.

"Hello. Everything all right with you and baby?"

"He's brutal. Kicks me day and night. Carter loves it, of course."

Alicia smiled, so glad for their happiness, so envious of it.

"Okay, I'm here now," Carter said from the other phone.

"How do you like your new job so far?" Sloan asked her.

She briefly outlined her new duties and responsibilities. Even to herself she sounded as excited as someone terrified of flying about to embark on a trip across the Pacific.

"It all sounds wonderful." Alicia could hear Sloan's forced enthusiasm. "Are you sure it's what you want? I mean—"

"She means you sound like hell. What's the matter with you?" Carter had never been known to mince words. And he knew all of them. "Are the boys all right?"

"They're fine." She told them about David's eye injury, leaving out Pierce, and reassured them that beyond having a faint scar his eye was fine.

"Well it sounds as though everyone is rocking along just dandy and peachy keen." Carter could also be sarcastic.

"Yes, we're fine." Alicia lapsed into silence, but her despondency came through the line loud and clear.

"Alicia, what's wrong?" Sloan asked with the quiet sincerity of an old friend.

Alicia drew in a serrated sigh. She wanted to cry. Her throat ached from holding tears back. It would be good to share it with someone. She didn't think she could bear the heartache alone any longer. "I met a man. A wonderful man."

"That's bad?" Carter asked. "Oh, wait, I know. He's not as good-looking as me. Right? Few are, darlin', but they can't help it. Don't let that get you down."

Alicia could appreciate his attempted humor and

laughed. "He's just as good-looking. But he's another type."

"Would we like him?"

"Yes." For the first time Alicia sounded animated. She described Pierce to them and had them laughing incredulously when she told them how she'd met him. "You should have seen us. We looked like three survivors of a shipwreck. David and Adam were blabbing all the family secrets to this total stranger. I was afraid for their lives and my virtue."

"But he turned out to be Prince Charming."

"Yes." Alicia blotted at the tears that were making mud of her eye makeup. "He was wonderful with the boys, so patient and entertaining. They loved him immediately. His daughter—"

"He's married?" Sloan asked.

"No, he's been divorced for years. His daughter is twenty-one. She's lovely. She came for dinner at the cabin one evening. We stayed the week with him, you see."

"So much for your virtue," Carter said, smacking his lips. "The plot thickens."

"Are you in love with him, Alicia?"

She gave up trying to hide the fact that she was crying. "Yes, yes."

"And how does he feel about you?"

"He . . . he said he loved me. I believe he did. He adored the boys."

"You're speaking in the past tense," Carter softly pointed out.

"We can't be together. We have . . . had a problem."

"What?" Sloan asked.

"He's a woman beater? An S&M freak? He moonlights as a pimp?" Carter's mind was always thinking up plot twists.

"No, nothing like that."

"Carter, please," his wife admonished gently. "Tell us, Alicia. What's keeping you and Pierce apart?"

"He's terminally ill."

Sloan murmured a soft, "Oh God, no." Carter's response was crude and considerably more explicit.

"At least there's a good possibility he is. Tests are being run now. It might turn out to be a treatable illness, but he's proceeding as though it's not. I must too."

The two calling from San Francisco were silent for a moment, then Carter asked, "Why?"

"Why what?"

"Why must you assume he's going to die and act accordingly?"

Defensively Alicia lashed back. "I've already lost one husband, Carter. If Pierce is dying—"

"We're all dying."

That took her breath. Her argument was stifled, corked in a quickly closing throat. "What? What are you saying?"

She could visualize him collecting his thoughts, Sloan sitting and listening quietly, which was her way. "Alicia, from the time we're born, we're all dying. Life doesn't carry any time-limit guarantees."

"But we don't live with the knowledge that it will happen at a given time."

"No, we don't. So why are you? You're not even sure that Pierce's condition is fatal. What if it isn't? The two of you are throwing away a damn good thing. Your reasoning is crazy."

"Carter," Sloan cautioned again. She knew that once he got wound up, once he set his mind to something, it was like trying to move a mountain to change it. "What did you say when Pierce told you?" she asked Alicia.

"Nothing, really. I was too shocked. I couldn't very well ask him to come back if he were going to live but to stay away if he were going to die." She moaned and covered her face with her free hand. "I would have begged him on bended kness to stay if it were only me. But how could I do that to my boys? They want a father so badly. How could they stand to lose Pierce like they did Jim?"

"Do you think they're better off without him at all, for any length of time?"

She thought over the last few days. They had been moving around as ghostly as she, their usual exuberance tamped out. They weren't happy. They were miserable. Their sulkiness was a silent accusation that she had driven Pierce away. "No, they miss him terribly. They love him."

"And what about you? Are you better off without him even if he is ill?"

She didn't even have to think to answer that one. "No."

"Alicia, let me ask you something," Carter said. "If you had known Jim was going to die when he did, would you still have wanted him for the time you had him? Would you have given up one single day you shared with him, one minute? Given the choice, would you have sacrificed having your sons with him, living with and loving him?"

"Oh, Carter." Crystal-clear realization of what he was asking dawned on her mind. "No, no, I wouldn't have. I would have greedily lived each day to the fullest."

"That's the way you should approach this. We only get one day at a time. Any of us. Are you living today the way you want to? Are you living it as though it were your last? What would you want to be doing if this were the last day of your life? Who would you want to be sharing it with?"

Pierce and David and Adam. She didn't even realize she had spoken the names aloud until she heard Sloan laugh softly and say, "Well then? What are you talking to us for?"

Alicia's body was surging with new life. She could hardly contain the energy suddenly gushing through it. "But he might not agree," she said nervously. "He might hold back, thinking we'd be better off in the long run."

"Convince him otherwise," Sloan said.

Alicia was laughing now. "Yes, yes, I will. I'll hang on until he gives in. Oh, I love the two of you. I love you."

"Tell that to Pierce. We already know you love us," Carter said.

"All right. Good-bye. I've got to go—"

"Call and tell us what happens," Sloan rushed to say.

"I will. Good-bye."

For a moment Alicia stood in the middle of the kitchen floor wringing her hands. There was so much to do, she didn't know what to do first. The dishes? They could wait. She had to get dressed.

She dashed toward her bedroom, repaired her makeup with fumbling fingers, threw on her clothes, and managed to pull herself into some semblance of order. Leaving a note for the sitter apologizing for the messy house, she ran for her car.

"I don't even know the address of Ecto," she said to her dashboard as she started out of her driveway. She slammed on the emergency brake, jumped out, wrestled with the key in the back door of the house, found her lost phone book, tore through its pages, ran back to the car.

Architecturally the office building looked like something out of *Star Wars*. She rushed inside, breathless, a rumpled whirlwind in the cool, dignified foyer. "Mr. Renolds, please."

"Third floor," the receptionist said. "The elevators are behind you."

"Thank you." She paced in front of the elevator doors as she waited, rehearsing what she was going to say when she saw him. He would argue. She needed ready ammunition to shoot down every argument.

There was a secretary sitting at a desk in the outer office. Behind her was a door with Pierce's name stenciled on it in gold leaf. "Mr. Reynolds, please."

The secretary looked puzzled and glanced down at the agenda on her desk. "Did you have an appointment?"

"No, but I think he'll see me. Tell him it's Alicia Russell."

"I'm sorry, Mrs. Russell, but Mr. Reynolds isn't here."

She stared stupidly. "Not here?"

"He called in this morning and said he wouldn't be in all day. If you care to make an appointment or see someone else . . ."

"No. No, thank you," Alicia said vaguely and turned away, retracing her way to the parking lot. She felt deflated. Lost. Aimless. A missile without a target.

Now what? Wait and see if he contacted her? No, no! She had to find him. Today. Now.

She got in her car and drove to the nearest public phone booth. There was no answer at his house. Chrissy was probably not home either. Didn't she have classes—

"Hello."

"Chrissy," Alicia gasped in relief. "Do you know where Pierce is? Is he by any chance with you?"

"No. He should be at his office."

"I've been there. He isn't working today."

"Is something wrong?"

"No, no." She didn't want to alarm Chrissy. "I just wanted to see him."

"Well, I'm glad to hear that. I talked to him yesterday and he sounded like a man in the depths of despair. He told me you weren't seeing each other anymore. I wish you two would get your act together and stop all this pussyfooting around."

Alicia smiled weakly. "I'm going to try. Beg if I have to."

"Good. I think he'd like to be begged a little. Something about middle-aged ego and all."

Middle-aged? "Well, sorry to have bothered you, Chrissy. I'll find him."

Alicia learned one thing from the conversation—Pierce was holding firm on his decision not to tell his daughter about his illness. Maybe he was right not to. But how could he stand the loneliness, the pain of facing something like that alone? He wouldn't. Not if she could help it. Alicia gunned the motor of her car and left the phone booth with a squeal of tires.

She parked outside the iron gates. The jeep he'd had at the cabin was parked at the side of the house, but his car wasn't in the driveway. He wasn't home. So she would wait. She rolled down the windows of her car.

*I'll wait for as long as I have to.*

She waited for hours, but she didn't mind. The time passed quickly as she closed her eyes and remembered. Everything. From the beginning. *"Mom, there's a man out there."*

The myraid ways she loved him were itemized and reviewed and counted again. When she saw the sleek foreign car prowling its way up the hilly road, she calmly got out of her car and was standing in front of the gate when he reached it.

His face was blank when he climbed out of the car. She went to him purposefully and confidently, wrapping her arms around his waist and laying her head on his chest.

"I love you, Pierce Reynolds. I need you with me for as long as I can have you. If it's forty years or four days, I've got to have you. Please stay with me."

His arms were like the strongest of steel bands as they closed around her. He bent his head over hers and pressed his lips into her hair. So close was the embrace that she could feel the steady beat of his heart against hers. "My love," he whispered fiercely. "My dearest, dearest love."

# *Ten*

"Can we have the cake now?" Adam asked.

"*May* we have the cake now. And, yes, you may."

"Give up on correcting his grammar, Carter," Alicia said. "I've tried. It doesn't work."

"He'll catch on, won'tcha, Adam?"

"Sure," Adam mumbled, his mouth full of birthday cake.

"Sloan, cake?" Carter asked his wife.

"No!" she exclaimed, warding off the enormous slice he offered her. "I'm trying to get my figure back."

"And succeeding," he snarled lecherously. "What about Jeffrey Steinbeck Madison? Can he eat cake yet?"

"*May* he eat cake," Adam chortled, and everyone laughed.

Alicia smiled as she held her friends' baby boy on her lap. She had only been introduced to him that morning when Carter and Sloan arrived for their visit. The patio party was in celebration of Jeff's three-month birthday. While Carter finished cutting the cake and passing slices to David, Chrissy, and a young man she had brought as her date, Alicia lovingly cooed to Jeff, who was somehow managing to sleep despite the commotion.

"I wish Pierce could have been here," Sloan said quietly as she sat down beside a subdued Alicia.

She sighed deeply and scanned the faces of those she loved collected around the patio table. "So do I, Sloan. He would have loved all this, the birthday cake, the children. He wanted to see your baby so badly."

Chrissy detached herself from the others and came to join Sloan and Alicia. "Don't be sad," she said, placing an affectionate arm around Alicia's shoulders.

"I'm not," Alicia said brightly, too brightly. "Honestly, I'm not."

Chrissy's smile wilted. "Well, I am. I miss Daddy being here."

Alicia took Chrissy's hand and squeezed it tightly in unspoken understanding.

Carter came over. He balanced a plate of cake in one hand as he squatted down in front of Alicia. "Are you going to eat this, or am I going to have to feed it to Jeff?"

Alicia laughed. "I'm not hungry, thank you anyway."

"Well, Jeff my boy, eat up." He scooped a generous portion of cake icing onto his fingertip and poked it into his son's mouth. Jeff began sucking and lapping noisily.

"Carter, don't you dare give that baby anymore," Sloan scolded.

"He likes it." Carter was totally enthralled with anything his son did.

"It will rot his teeth."

"He doesn't have any teeth."

"Oh. Well, when they come in they'll be rotten."

Alicia smiled at their bantering. They were so apparently happy with each other, so obviously in love. Again tears welled in her eyes.

"What's wrong, Alicia?" Sloan asked gently. Even Carter's cheerfulness faltered as he looked at Alicia's bleak expression. Chrissy's eyes, so like her father's, were clouded.

"I miss Pierce. God, I miss him so much. How can it possibly hurt this bad?"

"It will get better," Sloan said. Distressed over Alicia's sadness, she patted her back consolingly.

But there was no consoling her and they fell silent, listening as the boys grilled Chrissy's date on the Lakers' season.

"Did you save me a piece of cake?"

Alicia almost dropped Jeff as she jumped up and whirled around at the sound of his voice. He was framed in the back door, grinning broadly. "Surprise! I got away early."

"Pierce," Alicia breathed, heaving Jeff into Sloan's arms and launching herself toward her husband. "Pierce," she repeated as she crashed into him and they wrapped their arms around each other.

"Daddy! Daddy!" the boys shouted. Deserting their new friend, they clambered across the patio, hurdled outdoor furniture and Alicia's carefully cultivated begonias to throw themselves against Pierce's legs. Giving his wife an "I'll get to you later" smile, he knelt down and heartily hugged the boys. "Did you bring us something?" "We were good." "We didn't bother Mom, just like we promised you we wouldn't."

"Gosh, I missed you two rascals," he said, rubbing his hands over their dark heads affectionately. "And, yes, I brought you something. But first I want to visit with our guests and see the new baby."

With much fanfare, Pierce was introduced to baby Jeff. He kissed Sloan on the cheek and congratulated her on having a beautiful baby. "He gets his looks from his mother, of course," he said with affected malice as he shook hands with Carter.

The author laughed. "Still jealous of me, I see. Hey, what are you complaining about? You won her in the long run." The two men had met at the wedding and liked each other immediately. A strong friendship was developing. "Where have you been? Did Alicia say Atlanta?"

"Yes, I personally had to deliver a jet we had redesigned for a corporation. I couldn't rearrange the schedule they had set up. I'm sorry I wasn't here to welcome you when you arrived."

"I'm glad you showed up when you did. We've been through two boxes of Kleenex as it is," Carter teased, tugging on a lock of Alicia's hair. "I'd curtail the business trips for a while if I were you, Pierce. She can't handle your being away from her."

"This was the first time since we married." He kissed Alicia lightly. "Believe me, I got back as soon as I could."

"We didn't expect you at all," Chrissy said, wedging her way up to her father and hugging him enthusiastically. The awkwardness between them was no longer there. They were demonstrative in their feelings for each other. "Daddy, I'd like you to meet a fellow artist, John. He's a commercial illustrator."

Pierce shook hands with Chrissy's date. The two men appraised each other and apparently liked what they saw, for they both smiled congenially.

"I'm glad you got back," Chrissy said. "Alicia's been a basket case for three days. Not a whole lot of fun to be with."

"Were you weepy?" he asked, lowering his head confidentially.

"Yes," she answered softly. "How was Atlanta?"

"Cold and lonely." He spoke for her ears alone and pulled her close.

"But you talked to me on the phone last night."

"Not quite the same as having you in bed with me." He lifted a curl from her cheek and fingered it lovingly.

"You gave me no hope that you'd be back until Monday."

"I told them a bodacious lie this morning about my son cutting his eye at school and that I was needed at home."

"It wasn't quite a lie," she said, snuggling against him. "Whatever, I'm glad you're here."

"So am I." He cupped her jaw in his hand and tilted her face up for his kiss. His lips barely touched hers, and it wasn't near enough. Regardless of their audience, they turned into each other and lent themselves to a hungry kiss. When his tongue pressed into her mouth, she slid her arms around his neck.

Chrissy propped both fists on her hips in pretended agitation. "For goodness sake, you two, what is my new young man going to think?"

"I think he's got the right idea," John said and, taking hold of her wrist, led her away.

"Uh-oh," Adam said dismally. "We're never gonna get our presents now."

David was shaking his head with seven-year-old wisdom. "Once they start kissing, it takes them a long time to stop," he told Carter and Sloan solemnly.

"Does it?" Carter asked, smiling at Sloan.

"I've got to feed Jeff," she whispered and let her lips flirt with his ear.

"Goody. That's my favorite thing to watch," he said, his eyes lighting up.

"You're in charge of cleaning up the patio. Recruit David and Adam to help."

His face fell. "You're no fun, Sloan, no fun," he called

after her as she disappeared into the house, trailing laughter. As Carter passed Pierce and Alicia, still locked in their embrace, he muttered, "Show a little restraint, will you? You're making me horny as hell."

Gradually they pulled apart, their eyes simmering with awakened desires. The corner of Pierce's mouth tilted into a sexy grin. "I know the feeling."

Carter and Pierce cooked steaks outside while Alicia prepared the rest of the meal in the kitchen. It was about twice the size the one in her house had been and since her marrige to Pierce she had taken a renewed interest in cooking.

They ate in the dining room that until now had been used so infrequently. It was a boisterous meal. David and Adam loudly competed for Pierce's attention. Jeff set up a fuss until Sloan was forced to leave the table to change his diaper. John was as chatty as Chrissy and seemed not to be affected by the noise and confusion. He fit right in. Pierce and Alicia exchanged approving glances.

With far more chiefs than Indians pitching in, the kitchen was finally cleaned. Chrissy and John took their departure with promises to come back soon and to buy Carter's newest book. The boys were put to bed. Jeff was tucked into his portable crib. Since Carter's beach house was being remodeled to make room for the baby, they were talked into spending the night.

"You're sure you have room for us?" Sloan asked Pierce.

"For years I rattled around in this house all by myself. I can't tell you how glad I am to fill it up with people."

"I'm sure it seems to have shrunk since David and Adam moved in," Carter said, smiling.

Pierce reached for Alicia's hand. "I like it this way."

The Madisons retired to one of the guest bedrooms after sharing a last cup of coffee with Alicia and Pierce.

"Want me to wash your back?"

Pierce, water streaming over him, turned in time to see his wife of four months stepping into the shower with him. He reached for her and pulled her against him. "You have to ask?" His lips were on her neck, nuzzling, nibbling.

"Where's the soap?" she asked huskily. His hands slipped over her wet skin, found her breasts, caressed, teased, then stepped back to visually appreciate his handiwork.

He handed her the scented bar of soap. As they kissed, their mouths rapacious, she lathered her hands with soapy foam. Reaching around him, moving slowly, sensuously, she rubbed his back. Her breasts grazed his hair-matted chest.

"Miss me?" she asked. Her capricious tongue tested the distention of his nipples.

He groaned his pleasure. "Every minute. I was miserable."

"So was I." The skin of his back was sleek and wet under her palms. His waist was nipped in neatly, his buttocks were taut and firm. "Did you look at other women?"

"What women? There were no women in Atlanta." Her laugh soon became a tremulous sigh of desire. Lightly he squeezed the peaks of her breasts between his fingertips. He ripened them further with gentle flicks of his tongue.

"I'll bet women looked at you. You've got cute buns." Her hands honored the objects of her admiration.

He shrugged. "Maybe a few hundred gave me 'come on' glances. Can I help it if my buns are cute?" He let out a

yelp when Alicia smacked him with the palm of her
hand.

They laughed playfully but their mouths eventually
found each other beneath the steamy spray and melted
together in a mind-stealing kiss. His tongue caroused
rowdily. Her hands stroked down the backs of his thighs
as far as they could reach, then tiptoed up the insides.

He moaned, "Alicia?"

"Hmm?" Her mouth was busily tasting his, sipping
water from his lips.

"My front needs washing, too."

Taking up the bar of soap again she slowly worked up
another lather. She watched him through the mist
swirling around them, through the shower's spray, her
eyes telegraphing her body's sexual awareness of him.

She laid her hands flat on his chest and rubbed in
widening circles. She drew bubbly patterns on his chest
hair. The hard muscles were massaged with talented
fingers newly trained in the art. They worked their way
down his ribs, detailing each one. An indolent index finger traced that satiny arrow of hair down his stomach,
past his navel, into the dark thatch that housed his sex.
Her hands were slippery, wet, sinuous. He was hard,
warm, smooth.

Bending his knees slightly, he lifted her against him,
his hands supportive beneath her hips. Under the guidance of her hand, slowly, driving upward, he possessed
her.

She pressed his head against her breasts, unselfishly
giving of herself. He cradled her in his arms. The gentle
way he held her was in contrast to the turbulence of
their passion.

Long after the tumult came, they stood under the
spray, trembling with the aftershocks, vibrating with
love, until the water cooled their fevered bodies.

They lay facing each other in their bed, warm, drowsy seemingly sated. His emerald eyes roamed her face. Lazy fingers fiddled with strands of her hair.

"I love you," he stated simply.

"I know."

"Do you know how much?"

"I'm learning every day. I hope I never know the extent of your love because then the next day wouldn't be filled with discovery."

He kissed her palm and she felt his smile against it "You should quote that to Carter to use in one of his books. That's good."

She outlined his lips with her fingertip. "It's true. didn't know how much I loved you, how vital you are to me, until you went away." She combed her fingers through a clump of chest hair and kissed the contoured muscles beneath it.

"We won't ever be separated again."

She made a defeated sound and flopped over onto her back. "Oh, Pierce, I forgot. Next week I have to go to Dallas. A designer is having a trunk show there and I'm supposed to meet him and try to induce him to come to Glad Rags. And then that trip to New York is looming close."

His eyes traveled over her, feasting on her shape, the peachy texture of her skin, the delicacy of her frame, the lushness of her breasts, the allure of her femininity which was soft and downy and shadowy in the faint lamplight. "I'll invent business trips and go with you." He touched her breast, kissed it. His hand wandered lower.

She covered his caressing hand with her own, pressed it against her. "I was hoping you'd say that. We've rarely been alone since we got married."

"That weekend in the cabin with David and Adam doesn't count as a honeymoon?" he asked teasingly.

"Well, at least we shared the double bed that time." She laughed softly and laid her hand on his silvery-brown hair. "Few men would even want to date a widow with two rambunctious sons, much less marry one and take on that responsibility."

"I would have wanted you if you'd had ten sons. As for the boys being a responsibility, you know how I feel about that. They're a privilege, a gift I never expected to have. I love them."

"I know you do. You're a wonderful father. The best." She allowed his hands to wander at will over her body, lying still and compliant, basking in his obvious adoration. "Do you know what I love most about you?" he whispered.

"Yes, you told me once. My tush."

He chuckled. "No, I said that's what I was attracted to first."

"Oh, I stand corrected." She smiled, but she could see that he was serious.

"I love you most because you were willing to brave anything with me, even death." He laid his hand along her cheek and his eyes were shining as they delved into hers. "You speak to me of making a sacrifice in taking on the boys. But do you realize the sacrifice you were willing to make for me?" •

"I made no sacrifice by running after you, Pierce. It was a purely selfish decision. I wanted you, needed you, right then. I had to have you. Not out of necessity. I had learned to live on my own and take care of my family, but it was an empty achievement. I proved to myself that I could do it, but I didn't want to be alone. You were necessary to my spiritual self."

"It still took courage to come to me without knowing that the results of those tests were negative." Closing his eyes, he shook his head. "To think that I was at the doctor's office hearing the good news at the same time you were deciding you wanted me in any condition."

"In sickness and in health. Had the tests been positive, I still would have wanted you." She kissed him softly. "I'm just so very grateful to God that they weren't."

"So am I." He hugged her close. "From the first moment I saw you, I wanted to live to a ripe old age. wanted to have at least fifty years to look at your face."

She murmured his name against his lips before they kissed long and deep. Her thumbs stroked his cheekbones as they parted. "You'll have at least that long. The doctor said your blood irregularity is already clearing up with that medication he gave you."

He was surveying her body with hands sensitized to the feel of her. "If I get to feeling any heathier than I do right now, I'm going to die of overexertion." He pressed her back into the pillows and followed her down with his own body.

"Pierce," she protested on a sigh when at last he released her mouth to kiss her neck. "Making love in the shower where no one can hear us is one thing, but we have guests in the house, remember?"

Tenderly, but firmly, he clasped both her wrists in one fist and raised her arms above her head so that nothing restricted his view of her nakedness. He even moved aside stray tendrils of hair by blowing on them softly. His warm breath struck her skin in airy puffs that elicited goose bumps. With tantalizing leisure, he dragged his index finger down the underside of her arm to her breast. Whimpering softly, she raised her hips restlessly and shifted her legs against his. Each depraved movement belied her mild objections.

With his free hand, he cupped her breast and pushed it up slightly. A skillful thumb toyed with the nipple

"Carter and I made a pact. We're not to listen through our walls and they're not to listen through theirs."

"But Jeff is only three months old." She gasped as his tongue curled around the tip of her breast.

"You know what a creative mind Carter has." He drew her into his mouth and sucked gently. Her womb contracted with the sheer eroticism of his caressing tongue.

She had forgotten what they were talking about. His hands and mouth were tuning her to a fine pitch of desire. She knew the signals well by now, but they never failed to surprise her with their intensity. Each time they made love, it was unique and added another dimension to how much they loved each other.

"Open your thighs. Let me touch you," he murmured.

His hand glided down the smooth expanse of her stomach and abdomen. He fanned through the soft tuft of hair, then palmed the slight mound. Curving his fingers downward, he found her dewy with desire for him. "Oh, you're sweet," he breathed.

With loving, questing caresses he paid tribute to her womanhood. He watched as her eyes grew hazy with mounting passion. Lightly he scratched his evening-stubbled chin across her breasts, her stomach. His tongue sponged her navel as his fingers treated her to ecstasy.

"Pierce, love me."

"I am, my darling."

"Inside. Please, now!"

Draping her thighs over his, he slid his hands beneath her hips and lifted her to him. The velvety tip touched her, probed, was laved with her lotion. Then his hard fullness sank into her loveliness, deeper and deeper until he knew the sweetest entrapment.

Deftly stroking, he told her of his profound love. Whispered love words were poured in her ear, a chant that accompanied the undulating movements she arched to meet. His palms coasted down her sides, smoothed over her hips, thighs, then back up to fondle her breasts, which to him represented all that was sex, all that was woman, all that was love.

They clung to each other as the crisis thundered through them. It was riotous, but excruciatingly tender. Long after the crashing fury of it was spent, ripples of sensation shimmied through them.

He stayed, nestled deep. Raising himself, he gazed down into her eyes. The depths of love beckoned him and he drowned in them willingly. She reached up and touched his cheek, his hair, his mouth. Her voice was whiskey-flavored with emotion. "I never knew what it meant to really love until I loved you."

His fingers buried themselves in her hair. He kissed her eyebrows, her nose, touched her mouth with his. "I never knew what it meant to really *live* until I loved you."

And life and love were celebrated long into the night.

# THE SHAMROCK TRINITY

☐ **21975 RAFE, THE MAVERICK**
*by Kay Hooper*
$2.95

☐ **21976 YORK, THE RENEGADE**
*by Iris Johansen*
$2.95

☐ **21977 BURKE, THE KINGPIN**
*by Fayrene Preston*
$2.95

## THE LATEST IN BOOKS AND AUDIO CASSETTES

**Paperbacks**

| | | | |
|---|---|---|---|
| ☐ | 28416 | **RIGHTFULLY MINE** Doris Mortman | $5.95 |
| ☐ | 27032 | **FIRST BORN** Doris Mortman | $4.95 |
| ☐ | 27283 | **BRAZEN VIRTUE** Nora Roberts | $3.95 |
| ☐ | 25891 | **THE TWO MRS. GRENVILLES** Dominick Dunne | $4.95 |
| ☐ | 27891 | **PEOPLE LIKE US** Dominick Dunne | $4.95 |
| ☐ | 27260 | **WILD SWAN** Celeste De Blasis | $4.95 |
| ☐ | 25692 | **SWAN'S CHANCE** Celeste De Blasis | $4.95 |
| ☐ | 26543 | **ACT OF WILL** Barbara Taylor Bradford | $5.95 |
| ☐ | 27790 | **A WOMAN OF SUBSTANCE** Barbara Taylor Bradford | $5.95 |
| ☐ | 27197 | **CIRCLES** Doris Mortman | $5.95 |

**Audio**

| | | | |
|---|---|---|---|
| ☐ | **THE SHELL SEEKERS** by Rosamunde Pilcher Performance by Lynn Redgrave 180 Mins. Double Cassette | 48183-9 | $14.95 |
| ☐ | **COLD SASSY TREE** by Olive Ann Burns Performance by Richard Thomas 180 Mins. Double Cassette | 45166-9 | $14.95 |
| ☐ | **PEOPLE LIKE US** by Dominick Dunne Performance by Len Cariou 180 Mins. Double Cassette | 45164-2 | $14.95 |
| ☐ | **CAT'S EYE** by Margaret Atwood Performance by Kate Nelligan 180 Mins. Double Cassette | 45203-7 | $14.95 |

Bantam Books, Dept. FBS, 414 East Golf Road, Des Plaines, IL 60016

Please send me the items I have checked above. I am enclosing $_____
(please add $2.00 to cover postage and handling). Send check or money
order, no cash or C.O.D.s please. (Tape offer good in USA only.)

Mr/Ms _____

Address _____

City/State _____ Zip _____

Please allow four to six weeks for delivery.                    FBS–9/90
Prices and availability subject to change without notice.